Vinn's gaze flicked to Ailsa's mouth and back again to her eyes, the pad of his thumb moving against her lower lip in a soft-as-a-puff-of-air motion. "You want me. I want you. Some things never change."

Ailsa frowned. "But you told me before you didn't want to sleep with me. You said our reconciliation would be a hands-off arrangement—or words to that effect."

"Why not make the most of what's still between us?" he said.

"There's nothing still between us." Ailsa tried to pull away but his hold subtly tightened...and a part of her—a part she didn't want to believe existed anymore—clapped its hands in glee and cried, "He still wants you!"

Vinn's thumb gently pressed down on the middle of her lower lip, the most sensitive spot, where thousands of nerves were already firing off in anticipation for the pressure of his mouth. "Are you sure about that, *cara*?"

Melanie Milburne read her first Harlequin novel at the age of seventeen, in between studying for her final exams. After completing a master's degree in education, she decided to write a novel, and thus her career as a romance author was born. Melanie is an ambassador for the Australian Childhood Foundation and a keen dog lover and trainer. She enjoys long walks in the Tasmanian bush. In 2015 Melanie won the Holt Medallion, a prestigious award honoring outstanding literary talent.

Books by Melanie Milburne

Harlequin Presents

A Virgin for a Vow
The Tycoon's Marriage Deal
The Temporary Mrs. Marchetti
Unwrapping His Convenient Fiancée
His Mistress for a Week

One Night With Consequences

A Ring for the Greek's Baby

Wedlocked!

Wedding Night with Her Enemy

The Ravensdale Scandals

Ravensdale's Defiant Captive
Awakening the Ravensdale Heiress
Engaged to Her Ravensdale Enemy
The Most Scandalous Ravensdale

Visit the Author Profile page
at Harlequin.com for more titles.

Melanie Milburne

BLACKMAILED INTO THE
MARRIAGE BED

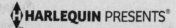

HARLEQUIN PRESENTS®

Recycling programs
for this product may
not exist in your area.

ISBN-13: 978-1-335-50425-8

Blackmailed into the Marriage Bed

First North American publication 2018

Copyright © 2018 by Melanie Milburne

Printed in U.S.A.

BLACKMAILED INTO THE MARRIAGE BED

To Franca Poli; thank you for being such a loyal fan. This Italian hero is for you, even though I know you already have one. xxxx

CHAPTER ONE

AILSA DECIDED THERE was only one thing worse than having to see Vinn Gagliardi after almost two years of separation, and that was being made to wait to see him.

And wait.

And wait.

And wait.

Not a couple of minutes. Not ten or fifteen or even twenty, but a whole stomach-knotting, nerve-jangling hour that crawled by like a wet century.

Ailsa pretended to read every glossy magazine Vinn's young and impossibly glamorous receptionist had artfully fanned on the handcrafted coffee table in front of her. She drank the perfectly brewed coffee and then the sparkling lemon-infused mineral water. She ignored the bowl of breath mints and chewed her nails instead. Right down to her elbow, and if Vinn didn't open his office door soon her shoulder would be next.

Of course he was doing it deliberately. She could picture him sitting behind his acre of French polished desk, idly passing the time sketching new furniture designs, a lazy smile tilting his mouth as he enjoyed every excruciating minute of the torture she was enduring out here at the prospect of seeing him again.

Ailsa squeezed her eyes shut, trying to rid her mind of the image of his smiling mouth. *Oh, dear God, his mouth.* The things his mouth had made her feel. The places on her body his mouth had kissed and caressed and left tingling for hours after.

No. No. No. Must not think about his mouth. She repeated the mantra she had been saying for the last twenty-two months. She was over him. Over. Him. There was a thick black line through her relationship with Vinn Gagliardi, and she had been the one to put it there.

'Mr Gagliardi will see you now.' The receptionist's voice made Ailsa's eyes spring open and her heart stutter like a lawnmower running over rocks. She shouldn't be feeling so…so nervous. What did she have to be nervous about? She had a perfect right to demand an audience with him, especially when it involved her younger brother.

Although…maybe she shouldn't have flown to Milan without making an appointment first, but she'd been in Florence for an appointment with some new clients when she got the call from her brother Isaac, informing her Vinn was going to sponsor his professional sporting career. She wasn't going to leave the country without confronting Vinn about his motive in investing in her brother's dream of becoming a pro golfer. She'd made up her mind if Vinn wouldn't see her today then she would damn well camp in his office building until he did. She had her overnight bag with her from her short trip to Florence so at least she had a change of clothes if it came to that.

Ailsa rose from the butter-soft leather sofa, but she'd been sitting for so long her legs gave a credible impression of belonging to a newborn foal. A premature newborn foal. She smoothed her damp hands down the front of her skirt, hitched her tote bag more securely over her shoulder and wheeled her overnight bag with the other hand, approaching the still closed office door with resentment bubbling like a boiling pot in her belly. Why didn't

Vinn come and greet her out here in Reception? Why make her walk all the way to his door and knock on it like she was some servile little nobody? Damn it. She'd been his wife. Slept in his bed. Shared everything with him.

Not quite everything...

Ailsa ignored the prod of her conscience. Who said husbands and wives had to share every single detail of their background? Especially with the sort of marriage she'd had with Vinn. It had been a lust match, not a love match. She'd married him knowing he didn't love her, but she'd convinced herself his desire for her more than made up for that. She'd convinced herself it would be enough. That *she* would be enough. But he'd wanted more than a trophy wife. Much more. More than she was prepared to give.

Ailsa was pretty sure Vinn hadn't told her everything about his background. He'd always been reluctant to talk about the time his father went to jail for fraud and how it impacted on his family's business. She'd soon got tired of pushing him to talk to her about it and let it slide, figuring she would hate it if he, or anyone for that matter, kept on at her to slide back the doors on her family's closet. She didn't have too many skeletons in there, just one big, stinking rotten carcass.

Ailsa stood in front of his office door and aligned her shoulders as if she were preparing for battle. No way was she going to knock on his door and wait for his permission to enter. *No flipping way.*

She switched her tote bag to the other shoulder and, grasping her overnight bag with her other clammy hand, took a deep breath and turned the knob and stepped over the threshold to find him standing with his back to her at the window overlooking the bustling streets of Milan. If that wasn't insult enough, he was seemingly engrossed in a conversation on his phone. He barely gave her a glance over his shoulder, just cursorily waved his hand towards one of the chairs opposite his desk and turned back to the view and continued his conversation as if she were some anonymous blow-in whom he had graciously shoehorned into his incredibly busy day.

A sharp pain seized her in the chest, his casual dismissal piercing the protective *I'm over him* membrane around her heart like a carelessly flung dart. How could he ignore her after not seeing her for so long? Hadn't she meant anything to him?

Anything at all?

The conversation was in Italian and Ailsa tried not to listen because listening to Vinn speak in his mother tongue always did strange things to her. Even when he talked in English it did strange things to her. She suspected even if he talked gibberish her spine would still go all mushy and every inch of her skin would tighten and tingle.

While he was talking she took a moment to surreptitiously study him…or at least she hoped it was surreptitious. Every now and again he would move slightly so she could see a little bit more of his face. It was as if he was rationing her vision of him, which was annoying in itself. She wanted to look him in the eye, to see if he carried any scars from their doomed relationship.

He changed the phone to his other hand and turned to the computer on his desk, his brow frowning in concentration as he clicked on the mouse. Why wasn't he looking at her? Surely he could show a bit more interest? She wasn't vain but she knew she looked good. Damn it, she paid a lot of money to look this good. She'd bought a new designer outfit for her meeting with her clients and had her hair done and had spent extra time on her make-up. Looking good on the outside made up for feeling rubbish and worthless on the inside.

Vinn moved something on the computer screen and then continued with his conversation. Ailsa was starting to wonder if she should have worn something with a little more cleavage to show him what he'd been missing. He was still as jaw-droppingly gorgeous as the last time she'd seen him. And if she hadn't been grinding her teeth to powder her jaw would be embedded in the plush ankle-deep carpet right then and there. His jet-black hair was neither long nor short nor straight nor curly, but somewhere sexily in the middle, reminding her of all the times she had trailed her fingers through those thick glossy strands, or fisted her hands in them during earth-shattering, planet-dislodging sex. He was clean-shaven but the rich dark stubble surrounding his nose and mouth and along his chiselled jaw was a heady reminder of all the times he'd left stubble rash on her softer skin. It had been like a sexy brand on her face, on her breasts, between her thighs…

Ailsa suppressed a shudder and, ignoring the chair he'd offered, threw him a look that would have frozen lava. In mid-flow. 'I want a word with you. Now.' She leaned on the word 'now' like a schoolmistress dressing down a disrespectful pupil.

The corners of Vinn's mouth flickered as if he were trying to stop a smile…or one of his trademark lip curls. He ended his phone call after another few moments and placed the phone on his desk with unnerving precision. 'If you'd made an appointment like everyone else then I would have plenty of time to talk to you.'

'I'm not everyone else.' Ailsa flashed him another glare. 'I'm your wife.'

A dark light gleamed in his espresso-brown gaze like the flick of a dangerous match. 'Don't you mean soon-to-be ex-wife?'

Did that mean he was finally going to sign off on their divorce? Because they'd married in England they were subject to English divorce law, which stated a couple had to be legally separated for two years. It was strange to think if they had married in Italy they would have been granted a divorce by now because Italian divorce law only required one year of separation.

'This may surprise you, Vinn, but I'm not here about our imminent divorce.'

'Let me guess.' He glanced at the overnight bag by her side and his eyes glinted again. 'You want to come back to me.'

Ailsa curled her hand around the handle of her bag so tightly her bitten-down nail beds stung. 'No. I do not want to come back to you. I'm here about my brother. Isaac told me you're offering to sponsor him for the international golfing circuit next year.'

'That's correct.'

She disguised a swallow. 'But…but why?'

'Why?' One dark eyebrow rose as if he found her question ludicrous and her imbecilic to have asked it. 'He asked me, that's why.'

'He…*asked* you?' Ailsa's mouth dropped open so wide she could have parked one of her brother's golf buggies inside. 'He didn't tell me that…' She took a much-needed breath and, letting go of her bag, gripped the back of the chair opposite his desk instead and swallowed again. 'He said you told him you would sponsor him but there were conditions on the deal. Conditions that involved me.'

Vinn's expression changed from mocking to masked. 'Sit down and we'll discuss them.'

Ailsa sat, not because he told her but because her legs were threatening to go from under her like damp drinking straws. Why had Isaac led her to believe Vinn had approached him over sponsorship? Why had her brother been so…so *insensitive* to invite her soon-to-be ex-husband back into her orbit? Vinn's involvement with her brother's golfing career would mean she wouldn't be able to avoid him the way she'd been doing for the last two years.

She had to avoid him.

She had to.

She didn't trust herself around him. She turned into someone else when she was with him. Someone who had all the hopes and dreams of a normal person—someone who didn't have a horrible secret in her background. A secret not even her brother knew about.

Her *half*-brother.

Ailsa was fifteen years old when she stumbled upon the truth about her biological father. For all that time she'd believed, along with everyone else, that her stepfather Michael was her dad. For fifteen years that lie had kept her family knitted together…well, knitted together was maybe stretching it a bit, because there were a few dropped stitches here and there.

Her parents, while individually decent and respectable people, hadn't been happy in their relationship, but she had always blamed them for not trying hard enough to get on.

She hadn't thought it was *her* fault.

That the lie about her was the thing that made their lives so wretchedly miserable. But after finding out the truth about her biological father and the circumstances surrounding her conception, she could understand why.

Ailsa straightened her skirt over her thighs and took a calming breath, but then her gaze spied a silver photograph frame on Vinn's desk and her heart stumbled like a foot missing a rung on a ladder. Why had he kept that? She had given him that frame after their wedding, with her favourite photo of them smiling at each other with the sun setting in the background. Giving him that photo had been her way of deluding herself she was in a real marriage and not one that was simply convenient for Vinn because he wanted a beautiful and accomplished wife to grace his home. She couldn't see the photo from her side of the desk. Perhaps he had someone else's image in there now. The thought of it churned her belly into a cauldron of caustic jealousy. She knew it was missish of her since she was the one to walk out on their marriage, but it hurt her pride to think he could so easily move on with his life.

And not just her pride was hurt...

Ailsa had always held a thread of hope that Vinn would fall in love with her. What bride didn't want her handsome husband to love her? She had fooled herself it would be enough to be his bride, to be in his bed. To be in his life.

But she had longed to be in his heart. To be the first person he thought of in the morning and the last he thought of at night. To be the person he valued over everyone else or anything else. But Vinn didn't value her. He didn't prioritise her. He didn't love her. Never had. Never would. He was incapable of it.

Vinn leaned back in his chair with one ankle crossed over his muscle-packed thigh, his dark unreadable gaze moving over her body like a minesweeper. 'You're looking good, *cara*.'

Ailsa stiffened. 'Don't call me that.'

His mouth curved upwards as if he found her anger amusing. 'Still the same old bad attitude Ailsa.'

'And why wouldn't I have a bad attitude where you're concerned?' Ailsa said. 'How do I know you didn't plant the idea of sponsorship in Isaac's mind? How often have you been in contact with him since we separated?'

'My relationship with your brother has nothing to do with my relationship with you,' Vinn said. 'That is entirely separate.'

'We don't have a relationship any more, Vinn.'

His eyes became obsidian-hard. 'And whose fault is that, hmm?'

Ailsa was trying to contain her temper but it was like trying to restrain a rabid Rottweiler on a Teacup Chihuahua's leash. 'We didn't have a relationship in the first place. You married me for all the wrong reasons. You wanted a trophy wife. Someone to do little nineteen-fifties wifey things for you while you got on with your business as if my career meant nothing to me.'

A tight line appeared around his mouth as if he too was having trouble reining in his temper. 'I trust your aforementioned career is keeping you warm at night? Or have you found yourself a lover to do that?'

She put up her chin. 'My private life is no longer any of your business.'

He made a sound that was suspiciously like

a snort. 'Isaac tells me you haven't even been on a date.'

Ailsa was going to kill her younger brother. She would chain him to the sofa and force him to watch animated Disney classics instead of the sports channel. She would take away his golf clubs and flush all his golf balls down the toilet. She would force-feed him junk food instead of the healthy organic stuff his sports dietician recommended.

'Well—' she gave Vinn a deliberately provocative look '—none that he knows about, that is.'

A muscle in the lower quadrant of his jaw moved in and out like an erratic pulse. 'Any lovers you've collected will have to move aside for the next three months as I have other plans for you.'

Plans? What plans? Now it was Ailsa's pulse that was erratic. So erratic it would have made any decent cardiologist reach for defibrillator paddles.

'Excuse me?' She injected derision into every word. 'You don't get to make plans for me, Vinn. Not any more. I'm in the driver's seat of my life and you're not even in the pit lane.'

He made a steeple with his fingers and rested them against his mouth, watching her with an unwavering gaze that made the hairs on the back of her neck prickle at the roots. But then she noticed the gold band of his wedding ring on his left hand and something in her stomach tilted. Why would he still be wearing that?

'Isaac will never make the professional circuit without adequate sponsorship,' he said after a long moment. 'That nightclub incident he was involved in last year has scared off any potential sponsors. I'm his only chance. His last chance.'

Ailsa mentally gulped. That nightclub incident could well have ended not just her brother's career prospects but his or someone else's life as well. The group of friends he'd been hanging around with since school attracted trouble and invariably Isaac got caught in the middle. It wasn't that he was easily led, more that he was a little slow to see the potential for trouble until it was too late to do anything—his approaching Vinn for sponsorship being a case in point. But if he got on the professional circuit he would be away from those trouble-making friends.

'Why are you doing this? Why are you involving me? If you want to sponsor him then do it. Leave me out of it.'

Vinn slowly shook his head. 'Not how it works, *cara*. You're the reason I'm sponsoring him. The only reason.'

Ailsa blinked. Could she have got it wrong about Vinn? Had he married her because he *loved* her, not just because he fancied having a glamorous wife to hang off his arm? Was that why he was still wearing his wedding ring? Had he meant every one of those promises he'd made on their wedding day?

No. Of course he hadn't loved her.

He had never said those three little magical words. But then, nor had she. She had deliberately held back from saying them because she hadn't liked the feeling of being so out of balance in their relationship. The person who loved the most had the least power. She hadn't been prepared to give him even more power over her than he already had. His power over her body was enough. More than enough.

He'd reeled her in with his charm and planted her in his life as his wife, on the surface fine with her decision not to have kids, but then he'd changed his mind a few months into their marriage. Or maybe he hadn't changed his mind at all. He had gambled on his ability to change her mind.

Gambled and lost.

She glanced at the photo frame again. 'Is that what I think it is?'

Vinn turned the frame around so she could see the image of their wedding day. Ailsa hadn't looked at their wedding photos since their separation. She had put the specially monogrammed albums at the back of her wardrobe under some clothes she no longer wore. It had been too embarrassing to look at her smiling face in all of those pictures where she had foolishly agreed to be a trophy wife. She had agreed to become a possession, not a person who had longings and hopes and dreams of her own. Looking at those photos was like looking at all the mistakes she had made. How could she have been so stupid to think an arrangement like that would ever work? That marrying anyone—especially someone like Vinn—would make her feel normal in a way she hadn't felt since she was fifteen? Their marriage hadn't even lasted a year. Eleven months and thirteen days, to be precise.

Vinn had mentioned the B word. A baby—

a family to continue the Gagliardi dynasty. She would have ended up a breeding machine, her career left to wither, while his business boomed.

Her interior decorating business was her baby. She had given birth to it, nurtured it and made numerous sacrifices for it. Having a real baby was out of the question. There were too many unknowns about her background.

How could she give birth to a child, not knowing what sort of bad blood flowed in its veins?

Ailsa swallowed against the barbed ball of bitterness in her throat and cast her gaze back to Vinn's onyx one. 'Why do you keep it on your desk?'

He turned the frame back so it was facing him, his expression now as inscrutable as his computer screen in sleep mode. 'One of the best bits of business advice I've ever received is never forget the mistakes of the past. Use them as learning platforms and move on.'

It wasn't the first time Ailsa had thought of herself as a mistake. Ever since she'd found out the circumstances surrounding her conception she had trouble thinking about herself as anything else. Most babies were conceived out of love but she had been conceived by brute force. 'What do your new lovers think when they see that photo on your desk?'

'It hasn't been a problem so far.'

Ailsa wasn't sure if he'd answered the question or not. Was he saying he'd had numerous lovers or that none of them had been inside his office? Or had he taken his new lovers elsewhere, not wanting to remind himself of all the times he had made love to her on that desk? Did he wear his wedding ring when he made love to other women? Or did he take it off when it suited him? She glanced at his face to see if there was any hint of the turmoil she was feeling, but his features were as indifferent as if she were a stranger who had walked in off the street.

'So…the conditions you're proposing…' she began.

'My grandfather is facing a do-or-die liver transplant,' Vinn said. 'The surgeon isn't giving any guarantee he will make it through the operation, but without it he will die within a matter of weeks.'

'I'm sorry to hear he's so unwell,' Ailsa said. 'But I hardly see how this has anything to do with—'

'If he dies, and there's a very big chance he will, then I want him to die at peace.'

Ailsa knew how much respect Vinn had for his grandfather Domenico Gagliardi and how the old man had helped him during the time when Vinn's father was in jail. She had genuinely liked Dom and, although she'd always found him a bit austere and even aloof on occasion, she could well imagine for Vinn the prospect of losing his grandfather was immensely painful. She wouldn't be human if she didn't feel for him during such a sad and difficult time, but she still couldn't see how it had anything to do with her.

'I know how much you care for your grandfather, Vinn. I wish there was something I could do to—'

'There *is* something you can do,' Vinn said. 'I want us to be reconciled until he is safely through the surgery.'

Ailsa looked at him as if he'd told her to jump out of the window, her heart thumping so heavily she could hear it like an echo in her ears. 'What?'

'You heard me.' The set to his mouth was grimly determined, as if he had made up his mind how things would be and nothing and no one was going to talk him out of it. Not even her.

She licked her parchment-dry lips. He wanted her back? Vinn wanted her to come back to him? As his wife? She opened and closed her mouth, trying to locate her voice. 'Are you mad?'

'Not mad. Determined to get my grandfather through this without adding to the stress he's already going through,' Vinn said. 'He's a family man with strong values. I want those values respected and honoured by resuming our marriage until he is well and truly out of danger. I will allow nothing and no one to compromise his recovery.'

Ailsa got to her feet so abruptly the chair almost toppled over. 'I've never heard anything so outrageous. You can't expect me to come back to you as if the last two years didn't happen. I won't do it. You can't make me.'

He remained seated with his unwavering gaze locked on hers. Something about his stillness made the floor of her belly flutter like a deck of rapidly shuffled cards.

'Isaac is talented but that talent will be wasted without my help and you know it,' he said. 'I will provide him with not one, not two, but three years of full sponsorship if you'll agree to come back to me for three months.'

Ailsa wanted to refuse. She needed to refuse. But if she refused her younger brother might never reach his potential. It was within her power to give Isaac this opportunity of a lifetime. But how could she go back to Vinn? Even for three minutes, let alone three months? She clutched the strap of her bag like it was a lifeline and blindly reached for her overnight bag, her hand curling around the handle for support.

'Aren't you forgetting something? I have a career in London. I can't just pack up everything and relocate here.'

'You could open a temporary branch of your business here in Milan,' he said. 'You could even set up a franchise arrangement. You already have some wealthy Italian clients, *sì*?'

Ailsa frowned so hard she could almost hear her eyebrows saying *ouch* at the collision. How had he heard about her Italian clients? Had Isaac told him? But she rarely mentioned anything much to her brother about her work. Isaac talked about his stuff not hers: his golfing dreams, his exercise regime, his frustration that their parents didn't understand how important his sport was to him and that, since their divorce, they weren't wealthy enough to help him get where he needed to be, etc. Ailsa hadn't told Isaac this last trip to Florence was to meet with a professional couple who had employed her to decorate their centuries-old villa. They had come to her studio in London and liked her work and engaged her services on the spot.

'How do you *know* that?'

Vinn's mouth curved in a mocking smile. 'I'm Italian. I have Italian friends and associates across the country.'

Suspicion crawled across Ailsa's scalp like a stick insect on stilts. 'So… Do I have *you* to thank for the di Capellis' villa in Florence? And the Ferrantes' in Rome?'

'Why shouldn't I recommend you? Your work is superb.'

Ailsa narrowed her gaze. 'Presumably, you mean as an interior decorator, not as a wife.'

'Maybe you'll be better at it the second time around.'

'There isn't going to be a second time around,' Ailsa said. 'You tricked me into marrying you the first time. Do you really think I'm so stupid I'd fall for it again?'

He leaned back in his leather chair with indolent grace, reminding her of a lion pausing before he pounced on his prey. 'I didn't say it would be a real marriage this time around.'

Ailsa wasn't sure whether to be relieved or insulted. Could he have made it any more obvious he didn't find her attractive any more? Sex was the only thing they were good at in the past. Better than good...brilliant. The chemistry they'd shared had been nothing short of electrifying. From their first kiss her body had sparked with incendiary sexual heat. She had never orgasmed with anyone but him. She hadn't even enjoyed sex before him. And, even more telling, she hadn't had sex *since* him. So why wouldn't he want to cash in on the amazing chemistry they'd shared?

'Not real...as in—?'

'We won't be sleeping together.'

'We...we won't?' She was annoyed her voice sounded so tentative and uncertain. So...crushed.

'We'll be together in public for the sake of appearances. But we'll have separate rooms in private.'

Ailsa couldn't understand why she was feeling so hurt. She didn't want to sleep with him.

Well, maybe her traitorous body did, but her mind was dead set against it. Her body would have to get a grip and behave itself because there was no way she was going to dive back into bed with Vinn… She had a sneaking suspicion she might not want to get out of it.

'Look, this is a pointless discussion because I'm not coming back to you in public or private or even in this century. Understood?'

He held her gaze with such quiet, steely intensity a shiver shimmied down her spine like rolling ice cubes. 'Once the three months is up I will grant you a divorce without contest.'

Ailsa swallowed again. This was what she'd wanted—an uncomplicated straightforward divorce. He would give it to her if she agreed to a three month charade. 'But if we're seen to be living together it will cancel out the last two years of separation according to English divorce law.'

'It will delay the divorce for another couple of years, but that would only be a problem if you're intending to marry someone else.' He waited a beat before adding, 'Are you?'

Ailsa forced herself to hold his gaze. 'That depends.'

'On?'

'On whether I find a man who'll treat me as an equal instead of a brood mare.'

He rose from his chair with an expelled breath as if his patience had come to the end of its leash. 'For God's sake, Ailsa. I raised the topic back then as a discussion, not as an imperative. I felt it was something we should at least talk about.'

'But you knew my opinion on having children when you asked me to marry you,' Ailsa said. 'You gave me the impression you were fine with not having a family. I wouldn't have married you if I'd thought you were going to hanker after a bunch of kids before the ink was barely dry on our marriage certificate.'

His expression was storm cloud broody and lightning flashed in his eyes. 'You have no idea of the word compromise, do you?'

Ailsa gave a mocking laugh. 'That's rich, coming from you. I didn't hear any talk of you offering to stay home and bring up the babies while I worked. You assumed I would gladly kick off my shoes and pad barefoot around your kitchen with my belly protruding, didn't you?'

His expression locked down into his trademark intractable manner. 'I've never understood why someone from such a normal and loving family would be so against having one of her own.'

Normal? There was nothing normal about her background. On the surface, yes, her family life looked normal and loving. Even since their divorce both her mother and stepfather had tried hard to keep things reasonably civil, but it was all smoke and mirrors and closed cupboards because the truth was too awful, too shameful and too horrifying to name.

On one level Ailsa understood her mother and stepfather's decision to keep the information about her mother's rape by a friend of a friend—who'd turned out to be a complete stranger gate-crashing a party—a secret from her. Her mother had been traumatised enough by the event, so traumatised she hadn't reported it to the police, nor had she told her boyfriend—Ailsa's stepfather—until it was too late to do anything about the pregnancy that had resulted. Her stepfather had always been against having a DNA test but her mother had insisted on it, saying she needed to know. When Ailsa was fifteen she had come home earlier than normal from school to overhear her mother and stepfather arguing in their bedroom. She'd overheard many arguments between her parents before but this one had been different. Overhearing the awful truth about her origin meant that her life and all her dreams and hopes for her own family had died in that stomach-curdling moment.

Ailsa met Vinn's flinty gaze. 'In spite of my refusal to play this game of charades with you, I hope you will still sponsor Isaac. He looks up to you and would be devastated if you—'

'That's not how I do business.'

She raised her chin a little higher. 'And I don't respond to blackmail.'

His gaze warred with hers for endless seconds, like so many of their battles in the past. It was strange, but this was one of the things she'd missed most about him. He was never one to shy away from an argument and nor was she. She had always secretly enjoyed their verbal skirmishes because most, if not all, of their arguments had ended in bed-wrecking make-up sex. She wondered if he was thinking about that now—how passionate and explosive their sex life had been. Did he miss it as much as she did? Did he ever reach for her in the middle of the night and feel a hollow ache deep inside to find the other side of the bed empty?

No, because his bed was probably never empty.

Ailsa was determined not to be the first to look away even though, as every heart-chugging second passed, she could feel her courage failing. His dark brown eyes had a hard glaze of bitterness and two taut lines of grimness bracketed his mouth, as if, these days, he only rarely smiled.

The sound of his phone ringing on the desk broke the deadlock and Vinn turned to pick it up. 'Nonno?' The conversation was brief and in Italian but Ailsa didn't need to be fluent to pick up the gist of it. She could see the host of emotions flickering across Vinn's face and the way the tanned column of his throat moved up and down. He put down the phone and looked at her blankly for a moment as if he'd forgotten she was even there.

'Is everything all right?' Ailsa took a step towards him before she checked herself. 'Is your grandfather—?'

'A donor has become available.' His voice sounded strangely hollow, as if it was coming through a vacuum. 'I thought there would be more time to prepare. A week or two or something but… The surgery will be carried out within a matter of hours.' He reached for his car keys on the desk and scooped up his jacket where it was hanging over the back of his office chair, his manner uncharacteristically flustered, distracted. In his haste to find his keys several papers slipped off the desk to the floor and he didn't even stop to retrieve them. 'I'm sorry to cut this meeting short but I'm going to see him now before—' another convulsive swallow '—it's too late.'

Ailsa had never seen Vinn so out of sorts. Nothing ever seemed to faze him. Even when she'd told him she was leaving two years ago, he'd been as emotionless as a robot. It intrigued her to see him feeling something. Was there actually a heart beating inside that impossibly broad chest? She bent down to pick up the scattered papers and, tidying them into a neat pile, silently handed them to him. He took them from her and tossed them on the desk, where a couple of pages fluttered back to the floor.

'I can't let him down,' he said in a low mumble, as if talking to himself. 'Not now. Not like this.'

'Would you like me to go with you?' The offer was out before Ailsa could stop it. 'My flight doesn't leave for a few hours so...'

His expression snapped out of its distracted mode and got straight back to cold, hard business. 'If you come with me, you come as my wife. Deal or no deal.'

Ailsa was torn between wanting to tell him where to put his deal and wanting to see more of this vulnerable side of him. She could agree to the charade verbally but he could hardly hold her to anything without having her sign something.

'I'll go with you to the hospital because I've always liked your grandfather. That's if you think he'd like to see me?'

'He would like to see you,' Vinn said and searched through the papers on his desk for something, muttering a curse word in the process.

'Is this what you're looking for?' Ailsa handed him the pages that had fallen the second time.

He took them from her and, reaching for a pen, slid them in front of her on the desk. 'Sign here.'

She ignored the pen and met his steely

gaze. 'Do we have to do it now? Your grandfather is—'

'Sign it.'

Ailsa could feel her will preparing for battle. Her spine stiffened to concrete, her jaw
set to stone and her gaze sent a round of fire
at his. 'I'm not signing it unless you give me
time to read it.'

'Damn it, Ailsa, there isn't time,' Vinn said,
slamming his hand down on the desk. 'I need
to see my grandfather. Trust me, okay? Just
for once in your life trust me. I can't let Nonno
down. I can't fail him. He's depending on me
to get him through this. Along with Isaac's
sponsorship, I'll pay you a lump sum of ten
million.'

Ailsa's eyebrows shot up so high she
thought they might hit the light fitting above
her head. 'Ten…*million*?'

The line of his mouth was white-tight. 'If
you don't sign in the next five seconds the deal
is off. Permanently.'

Ailsa took the pen from him, his fingers
brushing hers in the exchange, sending a riot
of fiery sensations from her fingertips to her
feminine core. The pen was still warm from
where he'd been holding it. She remembered

all too well his warmth. The way it lit the wick of her desire like a match on dry tinder. She could feel the smouldering of his touch moving through her body, awakening sensual memories.

Memories she had tried so hard to suppress.

She took a shaky breath and ran her gaze over the document. It was reasonably straight-forward: three years of sponsorship for Isaac and giving her a lump sum of ten million on signing. While it annoyed her he'd used money as a lure, she realised it was the primary language he spoke. Money was his mother tongue, not Italian. Well, she could learn to speak Money too. Ten million was a lot of money. She was successful in her business but with ten million in her bank account she could expand her studio to Europe.

But then she realised how trapped she would be once she signed that agreement. She would have to spend three months with Vinn. She needed time to think about this. She had rushed into marriage with him in the past. How foolish would it be to rush into this without proper and careful consideration? She left the document unsigned and pushed it and the pen back to him. 'I need a couple of days to think about this. It's a lot of money and... I need more time.'

He showed no emotion on his face, which surprised her given how insistent he had been moments earlier. But maybe behind that masked expression he was already planning another tactic to force her to comply with his will. 'We will discuss this further after we've been to the hospital.' He put the paper under a paperweight and, picking up her overnight bag, ushered her out of his office.

He spoke a few quick words to his receptionist Claudia, explaining what was happening, and Claudia expressed her concern and assured him she would take care of everything back here at the office. Ailsa felt a twinge of jealousy at the way the young woman seemed to be such an integral part of the business. She wondered what had happened to the receptionist who had worked for him during their marriage. Vinn liked surrounding himself with beautiful women and they didn't come more beautiful than Claudia, who looked as if she'd just stepped out of a photo shoot.

Ailsa waited until they were in Vinn's car and on their way to the hospital before she brought up the subject. 'What happened to your other receptionist, Rosa?'

'I fired her.'

She rounded her eyes in surprise. She'd thought his relationship with the middle-aged Rosa had been excellent. She'd often heard him describe Rosa as the backbone of the business and how he would be lost without her. Why on earth would he have fired her? 'Really? Why?'

He worked his way through the gears with an almost savage intensity. 'She overstepped the mark. I fired her. End of story.'

'Overstepped it in what way?'

He sent her a speaking glance. 'Could we leave this until another time?'

Ailsa bit her lip. 'I'm sorry... I know you're feeling stressed and this must be so upsetting for you with your grandfather so desperately ill...'

There was a long silence.

'He's all I have,' Vinn said in the same hollow-sounding voice he'd used back in his office. 'I'm not ready to lose him.'

She wanted to reach for his hand or to put her hand on his thigh the way she used to do, but instead she kept to her side of the car. He probably wouldn't welcome her comfort or he might push her away, which would be even worse. 'You still have your dad, don't you?' she said.

'No.' He made another gear change. 'He died. Car crash. He was driving under the influence and killed himself and his new girlfriend and seriously injured a couple and their two children travelling in the other car.'

'I'm so sorry…' Ailsa said. 'I didn't know that.'

It pained her to think Vinn had gone through such a tragic loss since she'd left and she'd known nothing about it. She hadn't even sent a card or flowers. Had he kept his dad's death out of the press? Not that she went looking for news about Vinn and his family…well, not unless she'd had one too many glasses of wine late at night when she was feeling particularly lonely and miserable.

He shrugged off her sympathy. 'He was on a fast track to disaster from the moment my mother died when I was a child. Without her steadying influence he was a train wreck waiting to happen.'

Ailsa had rarely heard Vinn mention his mother's death. It was something he never spoke of, even in passing. But she knew his relationship with his father had never truly recovered after his father was charged with fraud when Vinn was barely out of his teens. The shame on the family's name and the reputation of the bespoke furniture business had been hard to come back from, but coming back from it had been Vinn's blood, sweat and tears mission and he had done it, building the company into a global success.

'I guess not everyone gets to have a father-of-the-year dad,' she said, sighing as he turned into the entrance of the hospital. 'Both of us lucked out on that one.'

Vinn had pulled into a parking spot and glanced at her again with a frown. 'What do you mean? You've got a great dad. Michael's one of the most decent, hardworking men I've ever met.'

Ailsa wanted to kick herself. She even lifted one foot to do it, welcoming the stab of pain from her high heel because she was a fool to let her guard slip. A damn fool.

'Yes…yes, I know. He's wonderful…even since the divorce he still makes an effort to—'

'Then why say something like that? He'll always be your dad even though he's divorced from your mother.'

'Forget I said it. I… I wasn't thinking.' Ailsa hated that she sounded so flustered and hoped he'd put it down to the emotion of seeing his grandfather under such tense and potentially tragic circumstances. She had a feeling if he hadn't been in such a rush to see his grandfather before the surgery he might well have pushed her to explain herself a little more. It was a reprieve, but how long before he came back to it with his dog-with-a-bone determination?

It was a timely reminder she would have to be careful around Vinn. He knew her in a way few people did. Her knew her body like a maestro did an instrument. He knew her moods, her likes and dislikes, her tendency to use her sharp tongue as a weapon when she got cornered.

He didn't know her shameful secret, but how soon before he made it his business to find out?

CHAPTER TWO

VINN DIDN'T KNOW what was worse—seeing Ailsa again without a little more notice or walking into the hospital to see his grandfather, possibly for the last time. But, in a way, he'd been expecting to lose his grandfather... eventually. But two years ago when Ailsa called time on their marriage it had not only blindsided him but hit him in the chest like a freight train. Sure, they argued a bit now and again. What newly married couple didn't?

But he'd never thought she'd leave him.

They hadn't even made it to the first anniversary. For some reason that annoyed him more than anything else. He had given her everything money could buy. He had showered her with gifts and jewellery. Surrounded her with luxury and comfort, as was fitting for the wife of a successful man. He might not have loved her the way most wives expected to be loved, but she hadn't married him for love either. Lust was what brought them together and he'd been perfectly fine with that and so had she, or so he'd thought. She had never said the words and he hadn't fished for them. He'd just assumed she would be happy with the arrangement because most women wanted security over everything else and the one thing he was good at was providing financial security. Financial security was what you could bank on—*pardon the pun*—because emotions were fickle. People were fickle.

But Ailsa had been unwilling to even discuss the subject of having a child. He knew her career was important to her, as was his to him, but surely she could have been mature enough to sit down and discuss it like an adult? He'd told her he wasn't all that interested in having a family when they'd first got together because back then he wasn't. But after a few months of marriage, his grandfather had his first health scare with his liver and had spoken to Vinn privately about his desire for a grandchild to hold in his arms before he died. He had made it sound like Vinn would be letting down the family name by not providing an heir. That it would be a failure on Vinn's part not to secure the family business for future generations.

Letting the family down.

Failure.

With his father already the Gagliardi family's big failure, those words haunted Vinn. They stalked him in quiet moments. It reminded him of how close to losing everything he had been when his father had jeopardised everything with his fraudulent behaviour. Vinn couldn't allow himself to fail at anything. Being an only child had never really bothered him before then, but with his father acting like a born-again teenager at that time and his grandfather rapidly ageing, it had made Vinn think more and more about the future. Who would he leave his vast wealth to? What was the point of working so hard if you had no one to pass on your legacy to when you left this mortal coil?

But no, practically as soon as he'd brought up the topic, Ailsa had stormed out of his life like a petulant child, refusing to communicate with him except through their respective lawyers. She had dropped another failure on him—their marriage. He would give her the divorce when it suited him and not a moment before. He had far more pressing priorities and top of that list was getting his grandfather through this surgery.

Vinn was banking on Ailsa's love for her younger brother Isaac to get her to agree to his plan for the next three months. But her turning up unannounced at his office was a reminder of how careful he had to be around her.

Careful. Guarded. Controlled.

He'd assumed she would call and make an appointment, but the one thing he knew he should never do with Ailsa was assume anything. She had an unnerving ability to catch him off guard. Like when she'd point blank refused to sign his agreement even though he'd dangled ten million pounds in front of her. He hadn't expected her to ask for time to think about it. He'd expected her to sign it then and there. But with the pressure of getting to the hospital in time to see his grandfather before the surgery, Vinn had allowed her to get away without signing. He had never allowed anyone to do that to him before. Push him around. Manipulate him. He had always put measures in place to avoid being exploited or fooled or thwarted.

All through his life he had aced everything

he had ever set out to do, but his marriage to Ailsa was a failure. A big fat failure. How he hated that word—*failure*. Hated. Hated. Hated it. It made him feel out of control, incompetent.

But it wasn't just him who had been affected by Ailsa walking out on him. The breakup of their marriage had shattered his grandfather and it was no surprise the old man's health had gone into a steep decline shortly after Ailsa had left. The death of Vinn's father so soon after her leaving certainly hadn't helped. But in some ways his grandfather had coped better with Vinn's father's death than the breakup of Vinn's marriage. His marriage to Ailsa had been the hope his grandfather had clung to for the future—a future ripe with promise of a new generation, new beginnings and new success. But that hope had been snatched away when Ailsa left.

But just lately, as the two-year mark of the separation crept closer, he'd noticed his grandfather becoming more and more stressed and his health suffering as a result. His grandfather had always been a devoted family man and had stayed faithful and true to Vinn's grandmother, Maria, until her death five years ago. If Vinn could do this one thing—make his grandfather believe he and Ailsa were back together—then at least the old man's recovery wouldn't be compromised by the stress and worry about their imminent divorce.

Besides, this time around, Vinn would be the one in control of their relationship and he would stay in control. He wouldn't allow Ailsa to throw him over again. He had put a time limit on their 'reunion' and he'd mentioned the no-sex rule just to be on the safe side. When he'd seen her walk into his office unannounced, his loins had pulsed with a drumbeat of primal lust so powerful it nearly knocked him off his feet. And if he hadn't been talking to one of his senior staff on the phone about a tricky problem in one of his workshops, he might well have taken Ailsa into his arms then and there and challenged her to deny the spark that arced between them. The spark that had always arced between them from the first time they'd met at a furniture exhibition in Paris. He was attracted to her natural beauty—her long silky curtain of ash-blonde hair and creamy complexion and coltish model-like figure, and the way her bewitching grey-blue eyes seemed to change with her mood.

The other thing he'd liked about her back then was she hadn't been easy to pick up. With his sort of wealth and profile it had been a new experience meeting a woman who didn't dive head first into bed with him. She had taken playing hard to get to a whole new level. The thrill of the chase had been the biggest turn-on of his adult life. He had seen it as a challenge to get her to finally capitulate and, if he were honest, he would have to admit it was one of the reasons he'd married her instead of offering her an affair like anyone else. Maybe even the major reason. Because nothing shouted *I won* more than getting that wedding ring on her finger.

But that iron-strong determination of hers that had so attracted him in the first place was the same thing that had ultimately destroyed their marriage. She refused to back down over a position she adopted. It was her way or the highway and to hell with you if you didn't agree.

But Vinn was equally determined, and this next three months would prove it.

Ailsa followed Vinn into the private room where Domenico was being monitored prior to the transplant. Strict sterilisation procedures were being conducted and, according to the nurse, they would be a hundred times more stringent once the surgery was over.

The old man was lying in a bed with medical apparatus tethering him seemingly from every limb. He opened his eyes when Vinn approached the bed and gave a weak smile. 'You made it in time.'

Vinn gently took his grandfather's hand in his and Ailsa was touched to see the warmth and tenderness in Vinn's gaze. Had he ever looked at her like that? As if *she* mattered more than anything at that moment? She felt guilty for thinking such thoughts at such a time with his grandfather so desperately ill, but how could she not wish Vinn had felt something more than just earthy lust for her?

'I made it,' Vinn said. 'And I brought someone with me to see you.'

Domenico looked to where Ailsa was standing and his weary bloodshot eyes lit up like stadium lights. 'Ailsa? Is it really you?'

She stepped forward and put her hand on the old man's forearm, so close to where Vinn's hand was resting she felt a little electric tingle shoot up her arm. 'Hello, Dom.'

Dom's eyes began to water and he blinked a few times as if trying to control his emotions. 'My dear girl... You have no idea how much it thrills me to see you back with Vinn. I've prayed for this day. Prayed and prayed and prayed.'

Back with Vinn.

Those three words sent a wave of heat through her body and two hot pools of it firing in her cheeks. Had Vinn already told his grandfather they were back together? Had he been so arrogantly confident she would sign the agreement? She was glad now she hadn't signed it. Fervently glad. He had given her ten million very good reasons to sign it, but still, it rankled that he thought he could so easily buy her acquiescence by waving indecent amounts of money in front of her.

'But I'm not really—' Ailsa stopped midsentence. How could she tell Dom the opposite of what he clearly wanted to hear? She might not have signed Vinn's agreement, but his poor old grandfather was being wheeled into surgery within a matter of minutes for an operation, which he might not survive. What harm would it do to allow Dom this one moment?

She wasn't back with Vinn as in Back With

Vinn. She was playing a game of charades to keep an old man happy. Standing here by this old man's bedside with the prospect of his life with a clock ticking on it made her want to do everything in her power to make Dom feel settled and peaceful before his life-saving or, God forbid, life-ending surgery.

'I'm here,' she said and moved her hand so it was on top of Vinn's on Dom's hand. 'We're both here. Together.'

Tears dripped down from Dom's eyes and Ailsa leaned over to pluck a tissue from the box beside the bed and gently mopped them away, her eyes feeling suspiciously moist and her chest so tight it felt like she was having her own medical crisis.

'If I don't make it through this operation then at least I have the assurance you two have patched things up,' Dom said, his voice choked with emotion. 'You're meant to be together. I knew that the first time Vinn introduced me to you. You're a strong woman, Ailsa. And my grandson is a strong man and needs someone with enough backbone to handle him.'

Ailsa was going to handle Vinn all right. She was going to grab him by the front of the shirt and tell him what she thought of him manipulating her into this crazy charade by default. Even though she hadn't committed herself on paper, he must have known she wouldn't be able to help herself once she saw his desperately ill grandfather. No wonder he hadn't made a fuss back in his office when she'd refused to sign the wretched agreement. He had simply bided his time so he could play on her emotions because he knew it was her weak spot. Just like he was using her love and affection for her brother as a bargaining tool, forcing her to bend to his will.

'Time to go to Theatre,' a hospital orderly announced from the door.

Vinn leaned down to kiss his grandfather on both cheeks European style, his voice husky and deep. 'Good luck, Nonno. We'll be waiting for you once you come out of Recovery.'

If you come out of Recovery...

Ailsa could hear the unspoken words like a haunting echo inside her head. Vinn had lost his mother when he was a small child barely old enough to remember her. He had lost his grandmother—who had effectively raised him—five years ago, and lost his father during the last two years. Now he was facing the prospect of losing his grandfather. The grandfather who, in many ways, had been more of a father to him than his own father.

She hadn't expected to feel anything other than hate towards Vinn because of the way he had married her because he wanted a wife and she had somehow measured up to his standards. Little did he know how far below those standards she actually fell. But now she felt an enormous wave of sympathy for what he must be going through. She wasn't supposed to feel anything where Vinn was concerned. She was in the process of divorcing him.

But who wouldn't feel sorry for someone saying goodbye to a grandfather who had been there for them all of their life? Dom and his wife Maria had stepped in when Vinn's mother died when he was so young and again when his father had caused so much financial and emotional mayhem. Dom had been there for Vinn in every way possible and now he was facing the very real prospect of losing him. Not that she had found out any of that information about his grandparents' role in his life from Vinn. She had found out most of it from his previous secretary Rosa, who had filled her in on some of the Gagliardi family dynamics.

Ailsa leaned down to kiss Dom's cheeks and wish him well and, when she straightened, Vinn's arm encircled her waist and drew her close to his body. In spite of the layers of her clothes, his touch set off fireworks through her flesh. He was so much taller than she was and even in her high heels she barely came up to his shoulder. She had never been more aware of her femininity than when standing next to him. It was as if his body had secret radar that was finely tuned to hers, signalling to it, making it ping back responses she had little or no control over. She could feel them now. *Ping. Ping. Ping. Tingle. Tingle. Tingle.* The warm press of his hand on her left hip was sending a message straight to her core, like a network of fiery hot wires fizzing and whizzing. Her breasts began to stir, as if remembering the slightly calloused glide of his hands caressing them, his thumbs rolling over her nipples…

Ailsa gave herself a mental slap and eased out of Vinn's hold once Dom had been wheeled away, accompanied by the nurse and three other clinicians. She waited until they were alone before she turned to face Vinn with a skewering glare. 'Did you tell him we were back together before you'd even spoken to me?'

His expression showed faint signs of irritation. 'No. But he must've put two and two together when he saw you come in with me.' He rubbed a hand over his face, the sound of his stubble catching against his skin making something in her belly turn over. 'Thanks, by the way. You've made a frail old man very happy.'

Ailsa shifted her lips from side to side— a habit she'd had since childhood. She did it when she was stressed and she did it when she was thinking. 'But what about when he wakes up? He'll know there's something not right between us. He might be desperately sick but he's not a fool.'

His dark-as-pitch eyes moved between each of hers in a back and forth motion, as if looking for a gap in her firewall. 'You'll have to work a little harder on convincing him you're in love with me.'

Ailsa gave him an arch look. 'Maybe you could show me how to do it by example.'

His hooded gaze went to her mouth and something dropped off a shelf in her stomach. That was the look that had started their

crazy lust-driven relationship. The I-want-to-
have-jungle-sex-with-you look. The look that
melted her self-control like a scorching flame
on sorbet. But then, as if he remembered they
were still in a hospital room and likely to be
interrupted, he brought his gaze back to hers.
'I'm sure you'll do a great job once you see ten
million pounds in your bank account.' He took
out his phone and started pressing the keys,
adding, 'I'll transfer a quarter of the funds
now and the rest on signing.'

Ailsa bristled again at the suggestion she
could be bought. 'I don't care if you put twenty
million in my account, it won't change the fact
that I hate you. And I told you, I'm not signing
it until I've had time to think about it.'

He looked up from his phone with an unreadable look. 'Hate me all you like in private, *cara*, but in public—signed agreement
or not—you will act like a blissfully happy
bride or answer for the consequences.'

She ground her teeth together. 'Don't go
all macho man on me, Vinn. It won't work.'

One side of his mouth lifted in an indolent smile as if he was enjoying her strong
will colliding with his. He stepped closer and
lifted her chin with the tip of his finger. She

knew she should have jerked away from him but for some reason her body was locked in a mesmerised stasis. His eyes were so dark she couldn't make out his pupils and they pulsed with little flashes of heat that could have been anger or red-hot desire or a combination of the two.

'You really are spoiling for a fight, aren't you, *tesoro mio*? But you know where our fights end up, hmm? In bed with you raking your fingernails down my back as I make you come again and again and again.'

Ailsa could feel her cheeks blushing like an industrial furnace. How dare he remind her of how wanton she had been in his arms? He made her turn into an animal in his bed. A wild animal with needs and desires and hungers that had never been awakened, much less satisfied, by anyone but him.

The need to get away from him so she could think straight was suddenly paramount. She didn't care what agreement he wanted her to sign or for how much, but right then and there she had to put some space between them.

'Dream on, Vinn. I need the bathroom. Will you excuse me for a minute?'

'There's a bathroom in here.' He pointed

to the signed door in his grandfather's room. 'I'll wait for you.'

Ailsa gave him a tight smile that didn't show her teeth. 'Strange as this may seem given our previous relationship, but I would actually like a little privacy. I'll use the bathroom down the hall.' She moved past him and mentally steeled herself for him trying to stop her but she managed to escape without him touching her. She glanced back from the doorway but he had already taken out his phone and was tapping again at the screen.

Ailsa walked straight past the bathroom down the corridor and stepped into the first available lift. She would have taken the stairs but she was in too much of a hurry. She had left her overnight bag in Vinn's car but at least she had her passport in her tote bag. But then she began to weigh her options. If she flew back to London he would immediately withdraw his offer of Isaac's sponsorship. She had no reason to think he didn't mean every single word. She had run up against his steely will too many times to count. The only time she had won an argument with him was when she'd walked out on their marriage.

But in a way she hadn't really won.

She had left him almost two years ago but a secret part of her had hoped he would come after her. While on one level she accepted he didn't love her in the traditional sense, on another level she had been so desperate for a sign—any sign—he cared something for her that her walk out had been far more impulsive and dramatic than she'd intended. In hindsight, she realised she had been hormonal and moody and feeling neglected because he'd been working extra long hours. She'd felt like a toy that had been put to one side that no longer held its earlier appeal. When he'd mentioned having kids it had triggered all her fears about their relationship. It had triggered all her fears about herself. What sort of mother would she be? How could she risk having a child when she didn't know whose DNA she carried?

But Vinn hadn't come after her. He hadn't even called her. It seemed to prove how little he cared about her that he would let her call time on their marriage and not even put up a fight to beg her to stay.

But then, men like Vinn Gagliardi didn't beg. They commanded and people obeyed.

The lift doors opened and Ailsa looked towards the hospital entrance. Could she walk out those doors and hope some decent part of Vinn would make him go ahead with Isaac's sponsorship? But then she noticed a gathering of people outside and her heart began to skip in her chest. Paparazzi. Were they here for a visiting celebrity? It only took her a moment to realise *she* was the celebrity. Why hadn't she realised Vinn would contact the press about their 'reconciliation'? He was always a step or two ahead of her. It was as if he could read her mind as well as her body. She hadn't signed his stupid agreement so he had a Plan B and C and God knew how many others up his designer sleeve.

One of the paparazzo looked Ailsa's way and said something to his colleagues and then they came rushing through the front doors of the hospital.

Ailsa turned and stabbed at the lift button but when she looked up at the numbers she could see it was still on the fourth floor. She went to the next lift and, just as she pressed the button, the doors opened and she came face to face with Vinn.

He took her hand and looped her arm

through his. His expression was hard to read but the tensile strength in his grip was not. She would have to think twice before trying to outwit him. 'Our first press conference is about to begin,' he said. 'Nice that you could join me for it.'

Ailsa had no choice but to paint a plastic smile on her face as he swung her to face the press. The back and forth conversation was mostly in Italian so she could only pick up a few words here and there, but it was clear the press were delighted to hear the runaway wife of high profile billionaire furniture designer Vinn Gagliardi was back.

'Let's have a kiss for the cameras,' one of the journalists said in English.

Ailsa's heart began to race at the thought of Vinn's mouth coming down on hers, but he held up his hand like a stop sign. 'Please respect our privacy. This is a difficult day for both of us with my grandfather undergoing life-saving surgery. *Grazie.*'

The press gang parted like the Red Sea as Vinn led her towards the front doors of the hospital. She understood the gravity of the situation, with his grandfather hovering between life and death upstairs in Theatre, but why hadn't Vinn taken this opportunity to kiss her? Had she misinterpreted the way he'd looked at her mouth earlier? Was he really serious about the no-sex rule? Did it mean he already had someone in his life who serviced those needs for him? A sudden pain gripped her at the thought of him with someone else. For the last twenty-two months she had forced herself not to think about it. He was a man with a healthy sexual appetite. Not just healthy—voracious. He was thirty-five years old—in the prime of his life.

Vinn led her to where he'd parked his car and silently handed her into it. Ailsa knew he was angry. She could feel it simmering in the air like humidity before a storm. He got in behind the driver's wheel and gave her a look that would have blistered paint. 'You might not have signed the agreement yet, but you told my grandfather you're back with me. If you try to run away again I will not only withdraw my offer of sponsorship from Isaac, but I will make sure no one else ever offers to sponsor him. He won't be able to walk onto any golf course in Europe as a spectator, much less play in a tournament. Have I made myself clear?'

Ailsa would have loved to throw his agreement and his ten million back in his face. She would have loved to tear up the money note by note and stuff the pieces down the front of his shirt. But she loved her brother more than she hated Vinn. Much more. Which was kind of scary because she needed to vehemently hate him in order to keep herself safe. But could she ever be safe from Vinn? She raised her chin a fraction, unwilling to let go of her pride. 'You might think you can cleverly blackmail me back into your life for three months but I will always hate you. Ten million, twenty million—even fifty million—won't ever change that.'

'If I thought you were worth fifty million I would pay it.'

His words were as cruel and stinging as a slap and shocked and pained her into silence.

She watched out of the corner of her eye as his hands opened and closed on the steering wheel, his knuckles straining white against the stretched tendons. The air inside the cocoon of the car felt thick, dense, as if all the oxygen atoms had been sucked out.

Ailsa felt dangerously close to tears, which annoyed her because she wasn't a crier. She was a fighter not a crier. She gave as good as she got and never showed her vulnerability. She didn't like showing her neediness. She fought against her emotional weakness. She'd taught herself from a young age when her mother would turn away from her outstretched arms as if she couldn't bear to be touched, let alone hugged, by her own child.

Ailsa turned her head to stare blindly out of the window, vaguely registering people coming and going from the hospital. People going through the various cycles of life: birth, death, illness and recovery, sadness and happiness and hope and loss and everything in between.

Vinn released a heavy sigh and turned to face her. 'I'm sorry. That was…unkind of me.'

'Unkind?' Ailsa wasn't ready to forgive him. Her hurt was festering, pulsating and throbbing like a reopened wound. Old hurts and new hurts were twisting around each other like rough ropes tied too tightly against wounded flesh. 'But true in my case. I'm not worth anything to you. In fact, I'm surprised you offered ten million.'

He reached across the space between them and put a gentle hand to the nape of her neck where it seemed every nerve in her body had gathered to welcome his touch. 'I would pay any amount of money to get my grandfather safely through this surgery.' His mouth twisted in a rueful movement that wasn't quite a smile. 'I'm not ready to let him go.'

You were ready to let me go. The words hovered on the tip of her tongue but she didn't say them out loud. 'You really love him, don't you?'

His hand moved closer to the base of her scalp, his fingers moving through her hair sending shivers down her spine. 'He's family. The only family I have left.'

'Don't you have cousins and uncles and aunts and—?'

He made a dismissive sound. 'They ran for cover when my father's shady dealings became public knowledge. I have no time for fair weather family or friends.'

Ailsa hadn't realised until then how isolated he was. She knew there were numerous Gagliardi relatives because she had met a lot of them at their wedding. Some had refused the invitation because of his father's reputation but Vinn had shrugged it off as if it hadn't bothered him one way or the other. But where were they today, the day his grandfather faced the biggest battle of his life? Had anyone reached out to support Vinn? To offer comfort at such a difficult time? Who were his closest friends these days? She had met a few of his business associates in the past but none of them appeared to be close to him or he to them. He had a tendency to hold people at a distance.

And who knew that better than her?

Even though she had shared his body and his home for nearly a year he was as much of an enigma to her as ever.

Ailsa looked into his gaze and felt her resolve melting like an ice cube in a hot tub. She didn't have too many pressing engagements back in London. She had planned to have a week or two out of the studio to work on some designs for some clients at home. What would it matter if she rescheduled her flight for a day or two? Just until Dom got out of surgery or Recovery. Her assistant, Brooke, could handle anything urgent.

'How soon will you know if your grandfather is going to be out of immediate danger? I could stay in a hotel for a day or two... until I've made up my mind about the agreement.' Would he allow her that much leeway?

A day or two wasn't much of a reprieve but she needed to keep as much distance from him as she could—while she still could.

His hand moved further along her scalp, the glide of his fingers sending her senses spinning and her willpower wilting like a daffodil in the desert. 'Is it me you don't trust or is it yourself?' His voice was rich dark honey and gravel swirled together.

Ailsa could feel his body just inches away from hers, his tall frame like a powerful magnet, pulling her body, drawing it inexorably towards his. Her lips were suddenly so dry they felt like cardboard but she daren't moisten them because she knew Vinn would read that as a signal that she wanted him to kiss her.

Damn it. She *did* want him to kiss her. Wanted. Wanted. Wanted. But no way was she going to let him know that. She would get her willpower back into line. Right here. Right now. She glanced at his mouth. *Where the hell was her flipping willpower?* Why did he have to have such a beautiful mouth? Sculptured and firm and yet the lower lip had a sensual fullness to it that her mouth, and other parts of her body, remembered with a frisson of excitement.

Ailsa raised her chin and locked her gaze with his. 'You think I still want you?' She affected a little laugh. 'That ego of yours really is something, isn't it? I feel nothing for you. A big fat nothing.'

His eyes darkened and a knowing smile lifted one corner of his mouth and his fingers shifted back to her nape to toy with the underside of her hair. A sensation shimmied down her spine like a warm flow of melted caramel, gathering in a hot whirlpool between her thighs. His gaze went to her mouth and back to her eyes and back again as if he were in the process of deciding whether to kiss her or not. Every nerve in her lips prepared itself—leaping and dancing and clapping their hands in anticipation. Every cell of her body vibrated with a hum of primal longing as needs she had ignored, suppressed or denied for the last two years came to throbbing life.

But then he suddenly moved away from her and a mask came down over his features like a curtain lowering on a stage. 'Someone's waiting for this car space. We'd better get moving.'

Ailsa had completely forgotten they were still in the hospital car park. But that was typical of being in Vinn's company. She forgot stuff, like how he had only married her so he could tick the job of 'finding a wife' off his to-do list. She was a fool to think he still wanted *her*. Maybe he did physically, but that was a male thing. Men could separate the physical from the emotional far more easily than most women.

Vinn had never been emotionally connected with her. And she had been a fool to accept his proposal on those terms. He'd offered her marriage but she had a feeling that was only because she had been the first woman to resist him. He'd seen her as a challenge, a conquest, and putting a ring on her finger and having a big flashy society wedding had publicly broadcast his success in claiming her as his prize. Even if he hadn't loved her at the start of their marriage, she had been happy with his desire for her. It had been enough because no one had ever made her feel that way before.

Wanted.

Needed.

As if she was irreplaceable.

But if she had been so irreplaceable, surely he would have fought a little harder to keep her? She'd been let go without a whisper of protest. Sure, he'd been a little difficult over the divorce proceedings, but that was because of the wording of the pre-nuptial agreement. The fact that he'd insisted on a pre-nup was another stark reminder of the sort of marriage they had. She had ignored it at the time, telling herself that of course a man with that sort of hard-earned wealth would want to make sure it was well protected. She had dutifully signed the document, pretending she was happy to do so while a tiny alarm bell tinkled in the back of her mind. She'd slammed the door on it, but now the door was swinging wide open and the alarm bell was clanging with a warning.

Be careful.

CHAPTER THREE

VINN DROVE OUT of the hospital car park with his gut clenched around brutal balls of barbed wire. He would have stayed on the ward until his grandfather was out of surgery but he knew it would be many hours, and then even more, before Nonno was out of Recovery.

If he ever got out of Recovery.

He hated hospitals. Hospitals were places people you cared about went in and never came out. He had been young when his mother had come into hospital for routine surgery—four years old—but he'd been old enough to realise something was horribly wrong when the doctor came out to speak to his father. The look on his father's face was something he would never forget. But his father had lied to him, pretended everything was fine and that *Mamma* was coming home when she got better. It was the first of many lies his father had told him over the next few days, until his grandparents had stepped in and insisted he be told the truth.

Where would Vinn be without his grandfather? Nonno had been there for him through thick and thin and each and every one of his father's sins. He had stalwartly stood by Vinn, refusing to allow the shame of his father's behaviour to leave a stain on him.

And then when his father died, two days after Ailsa left, and the distraught family of those poor innocent victims had been baying for blood, Nonno had been steady and supportive, even though his grief at losing his only son must have been devastating. Vinn had mechanically organised his father's funeral and gave a short but respectful eulogy, but he'd done all of it like an automaton. He couldn't remember feeling anything during that time. He'd been blank. Like his motherboard had frozen. People had come up to him at the funeral expressing their condolences and casting their questioning gazes around for Ailsa. He'd made up some excuse for her absence, fully believing at that time she would be back.

But, in a way, his father's death had been

a good distraction from Ailsa walking out on him. It meant weeks, almost a month, had passed before he had to face the fact she wasn't coming back. He had assumed she would call him in a couple of days or text him, telling him she didn't mean it, that she was sorry and could they make up. She had often blown off steam like that and, once she got over her little temper tantrum, everything would return to normal.

But it hadn't returned to normal because she hadn't returned.

There had been no phone calls.

No text messages.

Vinn hadn't called her to inform her about his father's death. But then, why would he? She hadn't met his father and even Vinn rarely had much contact with him during their brief marriage. He'd assumed she'd find out from the press coverage, because there had been plenty of that at the time. Although the London tabloids didn't always carry what the Italian ones carried, which was a good thing as far as Vinn was concerned. The less the rest of the world knew about his father's shady dealings and the misery he'd inflicted on others the better.

But none of that mattered now because Ailsa was back and Vinn was going to make sure that when she left the second time around it would be on his terms not hers. He would get her to sign the agreement if it was the last thing he did.

Ailsa was expecting Vinn to take her to a hotel, but when he took the road that led to his villa in the upmarket district of Magenta she sent him a questioning look, her insides fluttering and flopping with panic…or maybe it wasn't panic. Maybe it was a feeling of excitement, but she refused to acknowledge it. She had no right getting excited around Vinn. That part of their relationship was over. Dead and buried over. 'I said I'll stay in a hotel, not with you.'

'Don't be ridiculous. What will the press make of that if they see you staying at a hotel now our reconciliation has been announced?' he said. 'It might get back to Nonno. You'll stay with me. It's the most sensible thing to do.'

Sensible? Nothing about being in the same country—the same geological era—with Vinn was sensible—never mind being alone with him in his villa. Not that they would be truly alone since he had a housekeeper and two gardeners. Ailsa had grown up with comfortable wealth—not rich, not poor but somewhere in between. But nothing had prepared her for the wealth Vinn had accumulated.

One of the things she'd enjoyed most about their brief months of marriage was how he'd let her decorate his villa. It had been her project—one of the biggest she'd done—and she'd relished the opportunity to bring the grand old beauty into full glory. Of course, she'd had to deal with the interference of Vinn's grumpy old housekeeper Carlotta, who'd always seemed to take issue with Ailsa over each and every change she'd wanted to bring about. But in the end Ailsa had ignored the old woman's comments and asides and got on with the job. It was her proudest achievement and, while she'd since removed the photos from her website, barely a day went past when she didn't think of the love and hard work she had poured into that beautiful old building.

Had Vinn changed it? Had he stripped every room of her influence? Purged the villa of her? Taken away every trace of her presence in his life? The thought of him undoing all of her work squeezed at her chest like a giant claw.

But then she remembered the one room that had triggered the final breakdown of their relationship.

The room that Vinn thought would make a great nursery. At first she'd thought he was joking, but day after day he kept bringing up the subject to the point where she would childishly plug her ears and walk away. She had planned to decorate the room as a guestroom with en suite bathroom and a lovely reading area near the windows overlooking the garden below. In the end she had left the room untouched.

She had closed the door on it and on their marriage.

'Same old Vinn,' Ailsa said, shooting him a murderous glare. 'Ordering me about as if I'm a child. But aren't you forgetting something? I haven't signed up for this. I'm only here for a day or two, max.'

He released a slow breath as if trying to remain patient. 'Can we just get through the next twenty-four hours without the verbal fisticuffs? I'm not in the mood for it.'

Ailsa remained silent until he pulled up outside the villa. Her chest was tight and her breathing shallow when he helped her out of the car and led her towards the front door. So many memories assailed her. He'd carried her over the threshold the day they returned from their honeymoon. Memories of making love in each room of the house in those first blissfully happy months. Kissing in doorways. Touching, wanting. This house was where they had their first argument…and their last.

Vinn opened the front door and silently gestured for her to enter. Ailsa stepped past him, breathing in the scent of him—the lemon and lime top notes of his aftershave with the base notes of something woodsy, reminding her of a deep, dark secluded forest.

She stepped into the hallway and it was like stepping back in time. Nothing had changed. The colours she had chosen, the furniture and fittings and little touches she had placed about were still there. Was every room still the same?

Ailsa swung her gaze back to his. 'I thought you would've gutted the place after I left. You know, got rid of my handiwork.'

He shrugged. 'Couldn't be bothered, to be frank.'

'Are all the rooms still the same?'

'Why wouldn't they be?' His expression was hard to read. 'I spent a fortune having it redecorated. I wasn't going to let the walk-out of my wife make me waste even more of my money.'

Ailsa could feel herself bristling like a cornered cat. 'I thought it was *our* money. We were married, for God's sake. Anyway, I spent a lot of my own money on this house because, unlike you, I don't have a problem with sharing.'

His eyes became hard, as if they had been coated with an impermeable sheen. 'I wasn't the one who forgot we were married, Ailsa. That was you.'

She blew out a whooshing breath, anger flooding her like a tide. 'Why is everything always *my* fault? What about your role in this? You shifted the goalposts, just like you did today. You overrode my opinions as if I hadn't spoken. You tried to force me to sign that stupid agreement and then you brought me here even though I expressly told you I wanted to go to a hotel. You don't listen, Vinn. You never have. You just do what you damn well want and to hell with anyone else's wishes. That's not how a marriage is supposed to work.'

His features had a boxed-up look about them, as if he was retreating inside himself. Or maybe it was more a case of him locking her out. 'I told you my reasons for bringing you here.'

'Yes, but we didn't discuss it first,' Ailsa said. 'You just got behind the wheel of your car and drove here, not once asking if it was okay with me.'

He rolled his eyes in a God-give-me-patience manner. 'Okay. We'll discuss it now.' He folded his arms and planted his feet as if he was settling in for a century or two. 'Talk to me. Tell me why you want to stay in a hotel.'

Because I don't trust myself around you. Because you're still the sexiest man I've ever met and I can barely keep my hands off you. Ailsa kept her expression masked. 'I prefer my own space. I've got used to it after the last twenty-two months.'

His gaze studied hers as if he was seeing through the lie like a detective saw through a false alibi. Then his gaze went to her mouth and something molten-hot spilled in her belly.

'Really.' He didn't say it as a question but in a tone that was faintly mocking.

Ailsa fussed with a loose strand of her hair, securing it back behind her ear for something to do with her hands in case they took it upon themselves to reach for him. A possibility that terrified her as much as it tempted her. Why was she so…so *weak* around him? It was like her body had no connection with her mind. It was running on autopilot and no amount of self-discipline or self-control had any impact.

'Yes. Really,' she said. 'I haven't missed you at all. Not a bit. In fact, on the contrary, I— hey, what are you doing?'

Vinn suddenly placed his hands on her hips, drawing her close enough for their lower bodies to touch pelvis-to-pelvis, heat-to-heat. Male to female. His eyes locked on hers, the slow burn of his gaze unravelling something tightly knotted in her body. 'You've always been a terrible liar.' One of his hands came up to cradle her face, his thumb moving over her cheek in a lazy caress that sent a frisson of electric awareness through her body. If her self-control had been in serious trouble before, now it was on life support. Nothing could have made her move away even though his hold was light.

No one had held her for the last twenty-two months.

No one.

Her skin craved human touch. She ached to be crushed to his body, to feel his warm male skin pressed to hers—to feel his mouth come crashing down to hers with its hot erotic promise. She fought the desire to close her eyes and lean into the hard heat of his tempting body. Need pulsed and pounded in each and every cell of her body, making her aware of every inch of her flesh. Flesh he had touched and teased and tantalised with such thrilling expertise in the past.

'I'm n-not lying.' Ailsa was ashamed her voice betrayed her with its wobble and whisper-softness.

Vinn's half smile switched off the ventilator on her self-control. His fingers splayed through her hair and his mouth came down to within a breath of hers, the sexy mingle of their breaths a heart-stopping reminder of other intimacies they'd shared. Intimacies she craved like an addict did a drug they had long been denied. Vinn was exactly like a drug—potent and powerful and with the unnerving ability to totally consume her.

Ailsa knew she should push him away. Knew it in her mind but her body was offline—it wasn't even in the same Wi-Fi zone. She even got as far as placing her hands on his chest but, instead of pushing, they fisted the front of his shirt until the buttons strained against their buttonholes.

'You think I still *want* you?' she said in a tone that was meant to be scornful but somehow sounded exactly like the cover-up it was.

His gaze flicked to her mouth and back again to her eyes, the pad of his thumb moving against her lower lip in a soft-as-a-puff-of-air motion. 'You want me. I want you. Some things never change.'

Ailsa frowned. 'But you told me before you didn't want to sleep with me. You said our reconciliation would be a hands-off arrangement—or words to that effect.'

He gave a lip shrug as if the prospect of sleeping with her was not much of an issue. Not for him maybe, but for her it was The Issue. 'Why not make the most of what's still between us?'

'There's nothing still between us.' Ailsa tried to pull away but his hold subtly tightened...and a part of her—a part she didn't want to believe existed any more—clapped its hands in glee and cried, *He still wants you!*

Vinn's thumb gently pressed down on the middle of her lower lip—the most sensitive spot where thousands of nerves were already firing off in anticipation for the pressure of his mouth. 'Are you sure about that, *cara*?'

Ailsa knew she had to resist him. She had to stop him kissing her. If he kissed her she was not going to be able to control herself. When had she ever been able to control herself when his mouth connected with hers? But with the tantalising presence of his thumb on her lips, she suddenly found herself parting them and tasting his salty skin with the tip of her tongue as if the connection between her rational brain and her body had been sabotaged. A bomb of lust exploded in his bottomless black gaze. The same explosion went off in her own body, sending flaming-hot darts of longing to sizzle in her core.

One corner of his mouth came up in a sexy slant. 'You really shouldn't have done that.' His deep voice was a silky caress in places that hadn't been caressed in so long Ailsa had almost forgotten what it was to be a woman. Almost.

She knew it was a mistake to moisten her mouth, but there was nothing she could do to stop her tongue sweeping over her lower lip where his thumb had rested. She kept her gaze locked on his. Not that she could have looked away if she'd tried. 'Why not?'

'Because now I have to do this.' And his mouth came down and covered hers.

His mouth was deceptively soft against hers, luring her into a sensual whirlpool in which she knew she could so easily drown. But the feel of his lips moving against hers with such exquisitely gentle pressure left her defenceless, disarmed and desperate for more. She made a sound against his lips—a whimpering, mewling, approving sound that betrayed her as shockingly as if she had shouted, *I want you*.

His tongue glided through her softly parted lips and rediscovered every corner of her mouth in deliciously arousing detail. The taste of him, the feel of him, the sheer maleness of him excited her senses into a madcap frenzy like someone poking at a hive of bees. Sensations buzzed through her flesh, hot prickles of want and cascading shivers of delight, and sweet little stabs of memory as his lips and tongue danced with hers like two ideally suited dancing partners coming together after a long absence.

Ailsa welcomed each stroke and glide of his tongue, relishing the way his breathing quickened and his hold tightened. At least she wasn't the only one who was affected. But it still worried her that one kiss could do this to her—turn her into a breathless, limbless wanton with zero willpower. She linked her arms around his neck and leaned into him, her breasts tingling at the contact with warm, hard male muscles.

Vinn slid his hands down to her hips, holding her against the potent ridge of his erection, his mouth making teasing little nips and nudges against hers.

'Want to do it here or shall we go upstairs?'

His blunt statement was a shot of adrenalin to her comatose willpower. Ailsa unwound her arms from around his neck and stepped back, throwing him a look that would have curdled milk. Long-life milk.

'Do you really think I would subject myself to more of your…your disgusting pawing?'

He made a soft sound of amusement and his eyes gleamed. 'You started it, *tesoro*. You know how hot I get for you when you use your tongue on me.'

Ailsa remembered all too well. Over the last two years she'd vainly tried to forget the things she had done with him. Wickedly sexy things she had not done with anyone else, or ever wanted to. It made her hate him all the more for being so damn...*special.*

She straightened her shoulders and looked down her nose at him like a haughty Victorian schoolmistress. 'I merely opened my mouth and your thumb was in the way.'

He gave a deep chuckle that made the floor of her belly shiver like an unset jelly. 'You're unbelievable.'

She forced herself to hold his gaze. 'Right back at you, buddy.'

He closed the distance between them and traced a slow pathway from the front of her left ear and along the line of her jaw, sending every nerve under her skin into raptures. His expression went from amused to serious. 'Thank you.'

It was such an unexpected thing for him to say it shocked her into silence for a moment. She looked at him in confusion. 'For?'

His fingertip traced a lazy circle on her

cheek, his eyes holding hers captive. 'For making me forget about Nonno for a while.'

Ailsa was a little shocked that she too had forgotten Dom. But hadn't it always been this way between her and Vinn? It was as if no one else existed when they were in each other's arms. 'Is it too early to call the hospital to see how he is?'

'Way too early.' His hand fell away from her face and went to scrape back his hair from his forehead instead. 'It will be hours and hours before we find out anything…' a worried frown flickered across his forehead '…unless, of course, something goes wrong.'

Ailsa put her hand on his forearm. 'Try not to think like that, Vinn. Your grandfather might be frail but they wouldn't have offered the surgery if they didn't think he had a fair chance.'

'He has no chance without it,' he said, releasing a sigh. 'No chance at all.'

She squeezed her fingers around the muscles of his forearm. 'Is there anything I can do?'

His eyes met hers. 'You're doing it by agreeing to come back to me.'

Ailsa dropped her hand from his arm as

if it had been scorched. 'I'll stay one night or two maximum. That's all. Just till he gets out of surgery.' *Or doesn't.* She didn't need to say the words out loud because she knew they were both thinking about the very real possibility that Dom wouldn't make it through the surgery. She crossed her arms over her body and glared at Vinn. 'You can't make me stay any longer than that. I haven't signed the agreement and I have commitments back home and—'

'Cancel them.'

'Oh, like you did during our marriage whenever I needed you?' Ailsa injected a stinging dose of sarcasm in her tone.

A brooding frown formed on his forehead. 'I run a large business that involves a lot of responsibility. I can't just take a day off to keep my bored wife amused. I have people relying on me for their incomes.'

'And why was I bored? Because you insisted I move to Milan and forget about my job back in London. I wasn't used to having so much spare time on my hands.'

'But you told me you were unhappy in that job,' Vinn said. 'You were working for someone else who was exploiting you.'

'Yeah, funny that,' Ailsa said with a pert tilt of her brow. 'I seem to attract those sort of people, don't I?'

His mouth flattened to a line of white. 'I did not exploit you. I told you what I was prepared to give you and—'

'And then you went and changed the rules,' Ailsa said. 'You thought you'd get me to pop out a baby or two while you go on with your terribly important career that can't be interrupted under any circumstances.'

'You are the most maddening young woman I've ever met,' Vinn said with a thread of anger running through his voice. 'It's impossible to discuss anything with you without it turning into World War Three. I've made it clear how this is going to work. I need you here for this week at the very least. I realise you have responsibilities back in London so I'll allow you to travel back and forth as needs be—'

'You'll *allow* me?' Ailsa could feel her eyes popping in outrage and her pulse thundering.

'I'm prepared to be reasonable.'

She laughed a mirthless laugh. 'Somehow you and the word *reasonable* don't fit too well together. I'll travel to London whenever I want or need to. I will not be ordered about by you, nor can you kidnap me.'

'Don't tempt me.'

Ditto. He was temptation personified. Putting her anger aside, Ailsa didn't know how she was going to keep her distance, and was privately impressed with herself for how she'd got this far without throwing herself upon him and begging him to make love to her. She blew out a breath and picked up her bag from where she'd left it on the floor.

'I need a cup of tea or something. Do you mind if I make myself one?' It seemed strange to be asking permission to do something in the home she used to call her own, but with the surly presence of his housekeeper Carlotta, no doubt still guarding her territory like a junkyard dog, Ailsa was reluctant to breeze in there as she had in the past. She didn't have the same rights and privileges now...but then, maybe she never had, which was something his housekeeper had made clear whenever she'd had an opportunity. Ailsa had tried to strike up a friendship with his housekeeper because she had felt a little daunted by being so far away from everything familiar. She had secretly hoped Carlotta would be a sort of

stand-in mother figure for her since her own
mother had never been the nurturing type.
But Carlotta hadn't been interested in con-
necting with Ailsa on any level. The older
woman had been cold and dismissive towards
any attempts on Ailsa's part to offer to help
around the villa. Ailsa had felt unwelcome,
a hindrance, an inconvenience. A burden to
be borne.

Just like she'd felt back at home with her
mother.

Vinn waved a hand in the direction of the
kitchen. 'Make yourself at home—you know
where everything is. I'm going out for a while.
I don't know when I'll be back. But call or text
me if you want me.'

That was the whole trouble—Ailsa did want
him. She wanted him so badly it was a persis-
tent ache in her flesh. When would she stop
wanting him? Would that day ever come? Or
had he left his mark on her like a brand? Making her his for ever by the simple fact of making her desire only him and him alone?

'What about Carlotta? Is she going to frog-
march me out of the house as soon as she sees
me or have you given her the heads-up?'

His mouth tightened as if he were recalling

all the arguments they'd had over his house-keeper's attitude towards her. An attitude he had never witnessed and therefore didn't believe existed. 'She's having the week off.'

'A week off? Wow, wonders will never cease.' Ailsa didn't bother pulling back on the sarcasm. 'I didn't think Carlotta had a life outside this house. She never even had a day off when I was here. Not once.'

He let out a breath that sounded faintly exasperated. 'I hope you're not going to make things difficult for her while you're here.'

'Difficult for *her*?' Ailsa laughed even though she felt like crying at the injustice. 'What about her making things difficult for me? I tried to get close to her and she shut me down like I was a stray dog who'd turned up at the back door looking for scraps.'

'Look, she's an old woman and I don't want—'

'She should've retired by now,' Ailsa said. 'She doesn't even clean the house properly. I was always going around after her, redoing stuff she'd missed, which I'm sure was another reason why she hated me so much. Why do you still employ her when she's obviously past it?'

He let out an impatient-sounding breath. 'She did not hate you.'

'Not while you were around, no,' Ailsa said. 'She saved it for when you weren't there to witness it. How old is she anyway?'

'Seventy-three.'

Ailsa widened her eyes. 'Seventy-three? That's surely a bit old to be still in full-time employment, isn't it?'

'She's been working for my family for a long time.' He paused for a beat and then continued. 'Since before my mother died. They were...close, or as close as a housekeeper and an employer could be.'

Ailsa tried to read his expression but it was like trying to read invisible ink. 'So you keep her on because of her link to your mother?' He had so rarely mentioned his mother in the past. She had tried to draw him out about what he could remember about his mother but she had got the impression he'd been too young when his mother died to remember much at all.

A shadow passed over his gaze but then his mouth became tightly compressed as if he regretted his uncharacteristic disclosure. 'Please—make yourself at home. I'll let you know if there is any news on Nonno.' And with that he turned and left her in the hallway with just the echo of his footsteps for company.

Ailsa made her way to the kitchen, but instead of making herself a cup of tea, she stood and looked out of the windows to the courtyard and garden beyond. The two-lane lap pool sparkled in the warm spring sunshine and, even without opening the French doors, she could almost smell the purple wisteria hanging in a scented arras.

How many other women had Vinn made love to in that pool? How many other women had he made love to under the dappled shade of those trees? Her stomach clenched into a fist of anguish.

How many women had he made love to in the bed he had once shared with her?

She turned away from the window and sighed. Why was she even thinking about things like that? She had been the one to leave their marriage. If Vinn had taken up with other women since, surely that was his prerogative? They had been separated almost two years. Longer than they'd been together. Two years was a long time to be celibate for a man who had been having sex since his teens. *Damn it.* It was a long time for her and she'd only been having sex—the sort of sex that was worth mentioning, that was—while she had been married to Vinn.

Ailsa left the kitchen and made her way upstairs to the master bedroom she had once shared with him. Even as she walked towards it, she knew she was inflicting unbearable torture on herself but she felt compelled to revisit that room, to see if anything had been changed. There were numerous other rooms she could have visited first, but no, her legs were carrying her, step by step, to that room.

She pushed open the door and for a moment just stood there, breathing in the faint scent of Vinn's aftershave that was still lingering in the air. The king-size bed was neatly made and she wondered again who was the last woman to sleep in it with him.

Ailsa swallowed a tight lump as she walked towards the walk-in wardrobe, drawn there like a hapless moth to a deadly flame. *This is going to hurt.* But, even as she mentally said the words, she pulled back the sliding doors…

CHAPTER FOUR

AILSA STOOD AS still as one of the marble statues in the garden below and stared at the rows and rows of her clothes. At first she thought they might have been someone else's but she recognised the fabrics, the styles, the colours. Things Vinn had bought her, expensive things—things she could never have afforded herself.

She'd stormed out in such a hurry that she hadn't bothered packing, mostly because a secret stubborn part of her had always hoped to come back when Vinn pleaded and begged her to, which of course he hadn't done. She hadn't asked him to return anything to her London address because, once it was clear he wasn't going to fight for her, she'd wanted to put her life with him in Milan behind her. She had wanted no reminders, no triggers for memories that could make her regret her impulsive decision to call time on their marriage.

For she could see now, with the benefit of hindsight, how impulsive it had been. How… how immature to storm out like a tantrum-throwing child instead of trying to work at better communication. Why hadn't she tried harder to understand where Vinn was coming from? If he'd wanted to talk about the possibility of having children then surely she should have been mature enough to have the discussion even if her opinion remained the same. It was becoming apparent to her that his inability to see the flaws in his housekeeper was deeply rooted in his attachment to Carlotta that stretched back to his early childhood. A childhood he had told Ailsa virtually nothing about.

Why hadn't he told her about Carlotta's connection with his mother before?

And why hadn't she made it her business to find out more about his childhood?

Because she hadn't wanted him digging about in her own.

Ailsa trailed her fingers through the silky fabrics on the velvet hangers, releasing a tidal wave of memories as the clothes moved past her fingers. Why hadn't he got rid of them? Why not toss them out in the rubbish or donate them to charity?

Why keep them here, so close to his clothes?

Ailsa slid the doors closed and let out a serrated sigh. How well did she know Vinn? She knew the way he took his coffee and that he absolutely hated tea. She knew what books he liked to read and what movies he liked to watch. She knew he had a ticklish spot at the backs of his knees and that he always slept on the right side of the bed—no exceptions.

But how well did she *know* him?

Was his keeping her clothes a sentimental thing or a tactical thing? What if he wanted her to believe he hadn't given up hope on her returning? What if this very minute she was being masterfully manipulated?

Anger prickled her skin like a rash. Vinn was ruthless—she had always known that about him. He detested failure. He saw it as a weakness, even as a character flaw. He wanted her back for three months to prove what, exactly? That she couldn't resist him?

Ailsa smiled a secret smile.

She would *show* him how well she could resist him.

* * *

Vinn paced his Milan office floor like a tiger on a treadmill. He wondered now if he should have stayed back at the villa in case Ailsa did another runner on him. She still hadn't signed the agreement. He might be considered a little ruthless at times but he could hardly force her to sign it. He could offer her more money but he had a feeling it wasn't about the money. It was about her wanting to stand up to him. She could stand up to him all she liked but he didn't want anything to compromise his grandfather's recovery.

He had to have her here with him, otherwise people would suspect it was all a ruse. He wanted his grandfather to believe he and Ailsa were back together. He'd seen the joy on Nonno's face when she'd walked into his hospital room. Vinn hadn't seen his grandfather so animated, so overjoyed since the day Vinn had presented Ailsa to him as his fiancée. His grandfather had always approved of Vinn's choice of bride, which had not surprised him because Ailsa was everything a man could want in a bride: beautiful and smart, accomplished and quick-witted—the downside of that being, of course, she was a little sharp-tongued. His grandfather liked strong women and no one could describe Ailsa as anything but strong.

But Vinn hadn't chosen Ailsa as his bride to gain his grandfather's approval. He had chosen her because he couldn't imagine a time when he wouldn't feel attracted to her. He had never felt such powerful chemistry for a woman before. The sexual energy she triggered in him was shockingly primitive. No one had ever pushed his self-control to the edge the way she did. He wanted her with a fierce, burning ache that pulsed in his loins even now. He had tried for almost two years to rid his brain of the images of her going down on him, the way her lips and tongue could undo him until he was weak-kneed and shuddering. He knew she still wanted him as much as he wanted her. He could feel it in the air when they were in the same room together. It changed the atmosphere. Charged the atmosphere until the air all but crackled with tension.

Vinn couldn't settle to work—not with his grandfather still on the operating table and his almost-ex-wife no doubt searching through the bedroom they'd shared during their marriage. He'd heard Ailsa's footsteps going up the stairs on his way out of the villa and knew it wouldn't take her long to see he had left her things in the wardrobe. It seemed a foolish oversight now that she was back. What would she make of it? Why hadn't he tossed the lot out? Or shipped it to her? *Damn it.* He could have got Carlotta to do it.

But no, he had left things as a reminder of what happened when he let his guard down. What they'd had together was not something he'd had with anyone else and he'd expected it to continue. He'd had great sex before, yes. He'd even enjoyed some great relationships, and had even thought one or two might go the distance, but it wasn't until he'd met Ailsa that he'd realised what he'd been missing. She was feisty and opinionated and while it annoyed him at times, it also thrilled him. Because of his wealth and influence, he was used to people dancing around him—people-pleasers and sycophants all wanting to get on his good side.

But Ailsa wasn't afraid to stand up to him. She seemed to relish the opportunity to not just lock horns with him but to rip his horns off and stomp on them and smile sweetly while she was doing it. He'd always liked that about her. Her drive and determination rivalled his and it secretly impressed him as few others impressed him.

But she had left him and it still rankled. It rankled like the very devil. He couldn't countenance failure. Failure was for people who didn't try hard enough, who didn't work hard enough, who didn't *want* hard enough.

He hated surprises. He was a planner, an organiser, a goal-setter. Things didn't just happen—he *made* them happen. Success didn't come about by pure chance. Opportunity knocked on the door of preparation, and that was why, when Ailsa's younger brother had asked him for sponsorship, Vinn realised he had a chance to turn things around so he was back on the winner's podium.

Blackmail wasn't a word he was comfortable using but he would use it if he had to. He wanted Ailsa back for three months. Back in his house. Back in his life.

And, even more importantly, back in his bed.

He wouldn't have made an issue out of it if he hadn't seen the raw desire on her face, felt it in her body, felt it in her mouth as it was fused to his. She might baulk at signing the agreement but he had other ways to get her to change her mind. Much more satisfying ways.

He smiled and silently congratulated himself. *You've got this nailed.*

Ailsa waited for Vinn to come back that evening but he simply sent a text to say he had an urgent matter to see to and not to wait up. She hadn't realised how much she had been looking forward to another showdown with him until the opportunity for it was taken away. Wasn't he concerned she might leave and fly back to London? She hadn't signed his agreement. Yet. She couldn't get that ten million out of her mind.

She had never been the sort of person motivated by money. She enjoyed the good living she earned and was grateful she hadn't grown up in abject poverty. But the thought of all that money and the good she could do with it was tempting. Not just to build and expand her business but to help others. There must be other children born of rape out in the community. Perhaps she could set up a counselling service or a safe place where they could talk about their issues. She could even offer to pay for her mother to have counselling, something her mother had always shied away from. But if the prohibitive cost of long-term therapy were taken away, perhaps it would help her mother finally heal?

But signing the agreement would mean she would be back in Vinn's life for three months. He thought he had her cornered. Wasn't that why he'd left her here unaccompanied tonight? He was confident she wouldn't leave. And if it hadn't been for his grandfather still undergoing surgery, she would have left.

Ailsa barely slept that night, not just because she was in one of the spare rooms instead of the bed she used to share with Vinn, but also because she was listening for his return. Every time there was a sound in the house she sprang upright, but each time it was just the villa creaking or a noise outside on the street. She kept glancing at her watch, her anger at him escalating as each hour passed. One o'clock. Two o'clock. Three. Four. Five. Why would he be at work at this hour? Or wasn't he at work? Was he with someone? Someone he had on standby to assuage his needs?

Needs Ailsa used to satisfy.

Her anger turned to hurt. Deep scoring hurt like someone had taken a blistering-hot blade to her belly. She curled up in a ball and rocked against the pain. Why had she allowed herself to get into this situation? Exposing herself to Vinn's power to hurt her like no one else had hurt her?

Somehow she must have slept but when she finally woke up around nine the next morning there was still no sign of Vinn. He texted her at about ten to let her know he was at the hospital with his grandfather. Had he been there all night? She wanted to believe he had been sitting by his grandfather's bed but would that be allowed? Wouldn't it be more likely he'd gone to spend the night with someone? Someone female?

It was later that following night when Ailsa realised she wasn't alone in the villa. She'd been listening out for the return of Vinn's car or the sound of the front door opening and closing, annoyed with herself for being on such tenterhooks. She had lost so much sleep over him and tied herself into such big choking emotional knots, she felt rattled to the core of her being. She was supposed to be over him. He wasn't supposed to have this sort of power over her now.

But when she heard sounds coming from

within his study she realised he must have come back without telling her. It infuriated her that he was treating her as if she were a houseguest he had no desire to interact with unless it was absolutely necessary.

Ailsa didn't knock on Vinn's study door but barged right in and stalked over to his desk, where he was sitting. 'How long have you been back? I've been waiting for you since yesterday. Did you not think it would be polite to tell me you'd come back? I thought we had a burglar.'

He leaned back in his chair with a squeaking protest of expensive leather, his expression as inscrutable as a MI5 spy's. 'And what were you going to do if there had been a burglar in my office just now?'

Ailsa hated how he always criticised her impetuosity. So she was a little impulsive? He'd liked that about her in the bedroom. He'd been delighted and dazzled by it. *Stop thinking about you and him in bed*. She decided it was time for a change of subject. 'Why are my clothes still in your wardrobe?'

'I've been waiting for you to come back and collect them.'

She sucked in a breath, trying to contain her

temper but it was like trying to stop a pot from boiling over while someone else was deliberately turning up the heat underneath. 'How long were you prepared to keep them?'

He picked up a gold ballpoint pen off his desk and clicked it on and off in a carefully measured sequence of clicks. On. Off. On. Off. 'As long as it took.'

Ailsa refused to back down from the challenge in his dark-as-night gaze. 'I might never have come back.'

Something glinted in the back of his eyes and his pen clicked again, acting as a punctuation mark. 'But you did.'

Ailsa ground her teeth so hard she was sure she would be on liquids for the rest of her life. 'You had no right to keep my things.'

'You didn't ask for them back.'

'That's beside the point.'

His gaze was unwavering on hers. 'Why didn't you?'

'I think you know why.'

'I don't.' Another click-click of the pen. 'Enlighten me.'

Ailsa compressed her lips. 'You bought me all that stuff. They were clothes to fit the role of trophy wife.'

'Are you saying you didn't like them?'

She had liked them too damn much. 'I'm not saying you haven't got good taste, I'm just saying you wanted me to act a role I was no longer prepared to play.'

He dropped the pen and pushed back his chair and stood, coming around to sit on the corner of his desk right near where she was standing. She was conscious of his long strong legs within touching distance of hers and the way his eyes were almost level with hers because he was seated. She considered moving but didn't want to betray how vulnerable she felt around him. She put her game face on and stared back into his quietly assessing gaze.

'When did you change your mind?'

Ailsa tried to keep her expression under tight control but she could feel her left eyelid flickering. 'About what?'

'About not wanting to be a trophy wife, as you call it.'

She tucked a strand of hair back behind her ear for something to do with her hands. How could she tell him she had never been happy in the first place? That their marriage was not the fairy tale she had longed for since she was a little girl. That she had only accepted his offer of marriage because it made her feel marginally normal. The white dress and veil, the congregation-packed church, the vows, the hymns, the traditions that made her—for a short time at least—forget she was the daughter of a faceless monster. That for the first time in her life she had felt wanted and needed by someone. Someone who could have had anyone but had somehow chosen her. 'We should never have got married. We should have had a fling and left it at that. At least then we could have parted as friends.'

His eyes held hers for a long heart-chugging beat before his gaze went to her mouth. Then he lifted his hand and drew a line from the top of her cheekbone to the centre of her chin, not touching her mouth but close enough for the sensitive nerves in her lips to get all excited in case he did. 'You don't think we could one day be friends, *cara?*'

Ailsa pressed her lips together to stop them from tingling. Her heart was thudding like a couch potato at a fun run and her resolve was nowhere to be seen. 'We've never been friends, Vinn. We were just two people who had sex and got married in a hurry and had more sex.'

His mouth shifted in a rueful manner and he slowly underscored her lower lip with his fingertip, just brushing along her vermillion border, creating a storm of longing in her flesh. His hand fell away from her face and his gaze met hers. 'Perhaps you're right.' He released a short sigh. 'But it was great sex, *si*?'

Ailsa wished they weren't talking about sex. Talking about sex with Vinn was almost as good as doing it with him. Almost. The way he looked at her with those dark, sexily hooded eyes, the way his body was so close but not close enough, the way his hands kept touching her as if he couldn't help himself. Talking about sex—about *their* lovemaking—made her want him so badly it was like an unbearable itch taking over her entire body. 'Yes, but that doesn't mean I want it now. Or ever. From you, I mean. We're practically divorced and—'

His hands captured both of hers and drew her so close to him she was standing between his muscular thighs. Everything that was female in her started cheering like cheerleaders at a grand final. Her hands were flat against his chest, her breasts pushed so tightly against him she could feel the ridges of his muscles against her nipples. 'You do want it. You want me. That's why you haven't had anyone since me.'

Ailsa made a vain effort to pull away. Well, maybe it was more of a token effort if she were to be perfectly honest. She didn't want to pull away. She wanted to smack her lips on his and rip off all his clothes and get down to business to assuage this treacherous need spiralling through her body. But some small vestige of her pride refused to allow her to capitulate so easily. 'I'm sure you've had dozens since me. How soon did you replace me? A week? Two? Or are we talking days or maybe even hours?'

His hands released her and he set her from him and stood from where he had perched on the corner of the desk. He went back around the other side of the desk as if he were putting a barricade between them. His expression was just as barricaded. 'Until our divorce is finalised, I consider myself still legally married.'

Ailsa looked at him in shock. 'What are you saying? That you haven't had anyone since me? No one at all? But I saw pictures of you in the press with...' She stopped before she betrayed her almost obsessional perusal of the press for any mention of him. She had even gone as far as buying Italian gossip magazines. Ridiculous. And expensive and practically useless since she couldn't read Italian.

'I have a social life, but I've refrained from getting involved with anyone until our divorce is done and dusted. I didn't think it would be fair to bring a new partner into such a complicated situation. Why are you looking so shocked?'

Ailsa tried to rearrange her features into blank impassivity. Tried but failed. 'I just thought you'd...you know...move on quickly.'

He straightened some papers on his desk that, as far as Ailsa could tell, didn't need straightening. His eyes met hers across the desk—dark and glinting and dangerously sexy. 'You mean for a man with my appetite for sex?'

The less she thought about his appetite for sex, the better. It was *her* appetite for sex that was the problem right now. She couldn't get it out of her mind. She couldn't get the ache out of her body. 'I never took you to be a man who'd be celibate for two days let alone almost two years.'

He gave a shrug. 'I've eased the tension in

other ways. If nothing else, it's been good for business. All that redirected drive has paid off big time.'

Ailsa couldn't get her head around the fact he hadn't replaced her. Not with anyone. She'd spent the last two years torturing herself with images of him making love with other women, doing all the things he had done with her, saying all the things he had said to her, and yet... he hadn't.

He'd been celibate the whole time.

But why? What did it mean? He had more opportunity than most men to attract another lover. Many other lovers. And since they were officially separated and in the process of divorcing, then why wouldn't he have replaced her with someone else? Few people these days waited until the ink was dry on the divorce papers.

She had been celibate because having sex with someone else had never even crossed her mind. She'd looked at men in passing but mentally compared them to Vinn and found them lacking. No one came even close. No one stirred her senses the way he did. No one made her feel more like a woman than he did.

Ailsa slowly brought her gaze back to his,

but somehow the knowledge that he had been celibate for so long only intensified the sexual energy that pulsated between them. She'd been aware of it before. Well aware. But now it was crackling in the air like static electricity. She ran her tongue over her suddenly dry lips, her chest fluttering as if there were a hummingbird trapped in one of her heart valves. Two hummingbirds. Possibly three. 'So…that explains why our kiss in the hallway got a little…heated…'

Vinn came back around from behind his desk and, standing right in front of her, slowly tucked a loose strand of her hair back behind her ear, just as she had done moments earlier. But her fingers brushing against her skin hadn't set her nerves abuzz like his did. Ailsa could feel her body drawn towards him as if he were an industrial-strength magnet and she was a tiny iron filing. 'Three months, *cara*. That's all I want. After that you can have your divorce.'

Ailsa watched his mouth as he spoke, her mind and her body seesawing over whether to accept his terms. If she didn't and left right now she would be divorced from him within weeks and free to move on with her life, leaving him free to move on with his. Isaac would miss out on his chance at a golfing career, but she could only hope that he would find another career. He was young, and who didn't change career a couple of times these days anyway?

But if she accepted the three months arrangement she would be back in Vinn's life.

And even more tempting…back in his bed.

Could she do it? Could she risk three months with him just to get him out of her system once and for all? It wasn't as if she was committing to for ever. He didn't want for ever…or so he said.

Just three months.

She could have all the sex she wanted with him. She could indulge in a red-hot affair that had a time limit on it so she didn't have to feel trapped or worried he would suddenly start talking about making babies. It was risky. It was dangerous. But it was so tempting—especially since she'd found out he hadn't replaced her.

What did that mean?

Ailsa slowly brought her gaze back up to his. 'Why are you doing this?'

He slid a hand under the back of her hair,

his fingers splaying through the strands, making her shiver in sensory delight. 'I told you—I want my grandfather to have a stress-free recovery.'

She swallowed back a whimper of pleasure as his fingers started a gentle massage at the nape of her tense-as-a-knotted-rope neck. 'This isn't just about your grandfather. It's about us. About this…this chemistry we have.'

He brought his mouth down to the side of hers, nudging against her lips without taking it further. 'So you feel it too, hmm?'

Ailsa couldn't deny it. Her body was betraying her second by second. She angled her head to give him greater access to her neck, where he was now leaving a blazing trail of fire as his lips moved over her skin, the slight graze of his stubble stirring her senses into a frenzy. Desire slithered in quicksilver streaks to all her secret places. 'I want it to go away.' Her voice was too soft and whispery but she couldn't seem to help it. 'It *has* to go away.'

His mouth came back to just above hers, his breath mingling with hers and making every reason to resist him slink away in defeat. 'Maybe three months together will burn it out of our systems.' He nudged her lips—an invitation to nudge him back.

Ailsa shuddered and slid her arms around his waist and placed her mouth on his, giving herself up to the flame of lust that threatened to consume them both. The heat of his mouth engulfed her, sending her senses spinning out of control. His tongue found hers in an erotic collision that made her inner core instantly contract with need. His lips moved on hers with an almost desperate hunger, as if he had been waiting for years for the chance to feed off her lips. She kissed him back with the same greedy fervour, her tongue darting and dancing with his, her body on fire, her blood racing, her heart giving a good impression of trying to pump its way out of her chest.

Vinn brought one of his hands to the front of her silky blouse, where her breasts were already aching for his touch. He skated his hands over her shape without undoing the buttons and her flesh leapt and peaked at the promise of more of his touch. He tugged her blouse out of her skirt with an almost ruthless disregard for the price she'd paid for it. He slid his hands up her ribcage to just below her breasts, the slightly calloused pads of his fingers sending her into a paroxysm of pleasure.

His mouth continued its magic on hers, drawing from it a response that was just as feverish as his. Their tongues duelled and tangoed in a sexy combat that triggered a tug and release sensation between her thighs. He reached behind her back and deftly unclipped her bra, freeing her breasts to the caress of his hands. Delight rippled through her as he took possession of each breast in his hands, his thumb pads rolling over the budded nipples until she was breathless with need. He brought his mouth down to one breast, licking and stroking her areola with his tongue, sending her senses into raptures before he did the same to the other breast. His stubbly jaw abraded her tender flesh but she welcomed the rough caress, relishing the marks he would no doubt leave on her skin because it would prove that they were really doing this and it wasn't just her imagination playing tricks on her.

'I want you.' His admission was delivered with gruff urgency that made her blood pound all the harder.

Ailsa was beyond speech and began to work at his clothes, not caring that buttons were being popped. She had to get her hands on his body. She had to get her mouth on his hot skin. She had to get her desperate, unbearable desire for him sated.

A phone began to ring but she ignored it, too intent on freeing Vinn's belt from his trousers. But then his hand came down and stalled her, and he reached past her to pick up his phone off his desk. 'Vinn Gagliardi.'

Even the way he said his own name made Ailsa want to swoon, especially with his desire-roughened voice making it sound all the more sexy. He continued the conversation in Italian and she gestured to him to see if it was news from the hospital but he simply shook his head and mouthed the word 'work' and turned slightly away to complete the call.

It made her feel shut out. Put aside. Put on pause, just like all the times in the past when his work took priority. Just like last night. Just like it would always be because she wasn't anything to him other than someone to have sex with when he wanted.

Ailsa did up her bra and tucked her blouse back into her skirt and finger-combed her hair into some semblance of order. She would have excused a call from the hospital, but a work-related call was a stinging reminder of where she stood on his list of priorities. She was a plaything, something he picked up and put down when it suited him. Hadn't it always been that way? She had fooled herself he would one day see her as more than a trophy wife. But he could have married anyone. She was nothing special and never had been.

Ailsa mouthed at him she would be waiting for him upstairs, feeling a glimmer of triumph when she saw the anticipatory gleam in his gaze. But she wasn't going to be upstairs waiting for him like the old days. She was going to leave while she still had the willpower and the sense to do so.

CHAPTER FIVE

AILSA SLIPPED OUT of the villa and once she'd walked a short distance she hailed a cab. 'The airport, thank you,' she said to the driver. She sat back against the seat and rummaged in her tote bag for her phone and her passport. She planned to book a flight on her phone on the way to the airport but when she looked at her screen she saw it was almost out of battery. Why hadn't she thought to charge it? Never mind. At least if she turned it off Vinn wouldn't be able to call her. She knew she should really be calling Isaac to explain and/or apologise about the bitter disappointment he was in for, but she couldn't face it just yet. She had to get a flight booked, which she would have to do once she got to the airport.

She dug deeper in her bag for her passport but she couldn't find it. She upended the bag and its contents spilled out onto the back seat of the taxi. She wanted to scream. She wanted to scream and pummel the seat until the stuffing came out. How could Vinn do this to her? It was virtually kidnap. He'd taken her passport. He'd actually taken it out of her bag without her permission. She had always known him to be ruthless but this was getting ridiculous. Why was he so determined to make her stay with him? Was it just about his grandfather? Or was this about revenge?

'Is everything all right?' the driver asked.

Ailsa pasted a frozen smile on her face. 'Erm, I've changed my mind. I think I'll go to a hotel in the city instead.' She rattled off the first name she could think of, where she and Vinn had once had a drink after seeing a show. She would have no choice but to go back to his villa to demand he give back her passport but she wasn't going back until the morning. She wanted him to spend a sleepless night—like she had last night—worrying about where the hell she was.

It would serve him damn well right.

Vinn had only just got his work colleague off the phone when his phone rang again. His heart jumped when he saw it was the hospital calling. He'd spent the night before at the hospital, sitting in the waiting room, wanting to be on site when his grandfather came out of Theatre. But there had been a complication with the surgery and the operation had gone on well into the night. He had finally left the hospital after speaking to the surgeon, once his grandfather was transferred to Recovery, but he knew it was still way too early to be confident his grandfather was out of danger.

He mentally prepared himself for the worst this phone call might bring. His skin prickled from the top of his scalp to the soles of his feet, dread chugging through his veins at the anticipation of bad news. 'Vinn Gagliardi.'

'Signore Gagliardi, your grandfather is doing as well as can be expected and is now out of Recovery and in ICU. It's still early days but he's stable at the moment. We'll call you as soon as there is any change.'

'*Grazie.*' For a moment it was the only word Vinn could get past the sudden constriction in his throat. Emotions he hadn't visited since he was four years old were banked up there until he could scarcely draw a breath. 'Can I see him?'

'Best to leave it until tomorrow or even the

day after,' the doctor said. 'He looks worse than he is and he won't know if you're there or not. We're keeping him on a ventilator for a couple of days to get him through the worst of it.'

Vinn put the phone down once the doctor had rung off. Things had changed a lot from thirty years ago, when relatives were often shielded from the truth out of a misguided sense of compassion. He wanted to know all there was to know about his grandfather's condition. He didn't want to be left in the dark like he had been as a child, expecting his mother to come home, excited at the thought of seeing her again, only to find out she was lying dead and cold in the morgue. Nothing could have prepared him for the shock and heartache, but he still believed if he'd been told earlier he would have handled it better. He hadn't even been given the chance to say goodbye to his mother. He hadn't been allowed to even see her. For years, too many torturous years, he had fooled himself into believing she wasn't actually dead. That she had simply gone away and would one day walk back in the door and reach for him with one of her enveloping perfume-scented hugs.

But of course she hadn't come back. His childish mind had struggled to cope with the enormous loss the only way it could by conjuring up an explanation that was far more palatable than a young mother in her prime going into hospital for routine surgery only to die five days later from complications.

Vinn gave himself a mental shake. He hated thinking about his childhood. The loneliness of it. The sheer agony of it. The sickening realisation that at four years old he was without a reliable parent. His father had never been an involved father so Vinn couldn't excuse him on the basis of his grief. His father had grieved, certainly. But, within a month of the funeral, he had a new mistress, one of many who came and went over the years. Vinn had learned not to show his disapproval or his own ongoing grief for his mother. He'd buried it deep inside, locked it away with all his feelings and vulnerabilities because it was the only way he could cope. His grandfather and grandmother had understood, however. They'd never pressed him to talk about it but he knew they were conscious of his deep inner sadness and made every attempt to make up for his father's shortcomings by always being there as a solid, secure and steady influence in his life.

Vinn was suddenly conscious of the quietness of his villa. Had Ailsa given up on him joining her? He hadn't intended being away as long as he had the night before but he hadn't been able to tear himself away from the hospital until he'd spoken to the surgeon in person. Was she still angry with him for leaving her so long? Wasn't her anger another sign she wanted him as much as he wanted her? He had been longer on the phone than he'd expected. Some smoking-hot sex with her was just what he needed to make himself forget the tragedy of the past. He smiled to himself, picturing her waiting for him, naked in the bed they had once shared. His body thickened at the thought of her silken golden limbs wrapping around him.

He took the stairs two at a time, anticipation making his heart race. But when he opened the master bedroom door, the bed and the room were empty. He swung to the en suite bathroom but it too was empty. He went through each of the spare rooms on that floor, wondering if she had chosen to wait for him in another room.

He went to the spare bedroom furthest from his that she'd apparently slept in the night before and that was when he saw her passport lying almost out of sight next to the bed. Had she dropped it and inadvertently kicked it further out of sight? He picked it up and flicked through the pages. She had been to Italy four times since their separation, but then he already knew that because he had sent her clients to make sure she came back. He'd liked the thought of her returning to the scene of the crime, so to speak. To remind her of everything she had thrown away by walking out on him.

Vinn slipped the passport into his pocket and took out his phone to call her. If she were still in the villa at least he would hear it ringing. He didn't hear it and within seconds it went through to the message service. Before he could think what to do next a text message came through, but it wasn't from Ailsa. It was from an acquaintance of his who owned a luxury hotel in the centre of Milan, informing him that Ailsa had just checked in for the night. Nico Di Sante had heard the news of their reconciliation in the press the day before and wondered if anything was amiss.

Vinn quickly replied, telling him everything was fine and that he would be joining Ailsa shortly, but to keep it a secret as he wanted to surprise her because she thought he was still caught up with work.

Vinn wanted to do more than surprise her. He was going to put the wedding and engagement rings she'd left behind two years ago back on her finger and that was where they would stay until he gave her permission to remove them. She knew the terms. If she didn't sign the agreement her brother's golfing career would be over before it began. He wouldn't sabotage her brother's career as he'd threatened. The boy deserved a chance even if Vinn wouldn't end up being the one to give it to him. Isaac was typical of other lads his age, dreaming of the big time without putting in the hard yards. He liked the boy and thought he had genuine potential but there was no way Vinn was going to get screwed around by Ailsa. Not again. Had he misjudged her love for her brother? Did she hate him more than she loved Isaac?

He didn't care if she hated him or not. A bit of hate never got in the way of good sex.

As far as he was concerned, the more hate the better.

And right now he was damn near boiling with it.

Ailsa lay back in the luxury hotel bath that was as big as a swimming pool and sipped the complimentary champagne that had been delivered to the door a short time ago. It was a frightfully expensive show of defiance. She had never paid so much for a night's accommodation before but she figured it was worth it for one night of freedom before Vinn made her toe the line. Because, of course, she would have to do as he commanded.

Commanded, not asked. *Argh*.

She had thought about it long and hard. She couldn't let Isaac's chance slip away from him. After all, she knew what it felt like to give up on a dream. It hurt. The hurt and disappointment never went away. It sat like a weight in her chest, dragging her spirits down like a battleship's anchor.

You can't have what you want. You can never have what you want.

The words tortured her every time she heard them inside her head. Ailsa topped up her champagne glass. So what if she was getting tipsy and maudlin? So what if she felt sad and lonely and worthless? She was considering whether to have a good old self-pitying cry when the door of the bathroom suddenly opened and Vinn stood framed in the doorway. She gasped and drew her knees up to her chest, her heart knocking against her chest wall like a pendulum in an earthquake. 'How did you find me?'

His gaze raked her partially naked breasts—partially because of the amount of bubble bath she had poured into the water. 'Don't push me too far, *cara*. You know how it will end.'

Ailsa put up her chin and sent him a look as icy as the North Sea in winter. 'You stole my passport.'

'I did not steal your passport.' He took something out of his top pocket and handed it to her. 'I found it on the floor next to the bed in the spare bedroom.'

Ailsa took the passport with a bubble-coated hand and put it to one side on a marble shelf next to the bath. 'I don't believe you.'

He shrugged as if that didn't concern him. 'It's the truth whether you believe it or not.'

Ailsa wasn't sure what to think. She

wouldn't put it past him to have taken her passport, but she also knew her tendency to lose things. She was clumsy and careless under stress and being anywhere near Vinn created more stress than she could handle.

He pulled out a folded document from his back pocket and, using one of the glossy magazines she'd brought into the bathroom as a firm backing, he unfolded it before handing her a pen. 'Sign it.'

Ailsa wished she had the courage to push the wretched document into the bathwater. She wanted to make it dissolve until it was nothing but flotsam floating around her. She wanted to take his stupid gold pen and stab him in the eyes with it. But instead she took the pen and, giving him a beady look, signed her name with an exaggerated flourish. 'Happy now?'

He folded the document and put it to one side and then put his hand back in his trouser pocket and took out the ring box she'd left behind two years ago. 'I want you to wear these until the three months is over.' There was something about his voice that warned her she would be wise to put the rings back on her finger without an argument, even though it went against her nature to be told what to do.

She took the rings from the box and slipped them on her finger, shooting him another glare. She didn't want to let him know how much she'd missed wearing those rings. The engagement ring was the most beautiful she had ever seen. He'd had it designed specially for her and, while he had never told her how much it cost, she had a feeling it was more than what most people earned in a lifetime. But it wasn't the ring's value she loved. She would have been happy with a cheap ring if he had given it to her with his love. He started to undo his shirt buttons and she reared back in horror. 'What are you doing?'

'We were interrupted an hour or so ago.' His shirt dropped to the floor and his hands went to the waistband of his trousers. 'I was telling you how much I wanted you, remember?'

Ailsa wished she hadn't drunk so much champagne. Her willpower was never a match for Vinn's charm but with alcohol on board it was as good as useless. 'You were telling me how much you wanted me, yes. But, you might recall, I didn't say it back to you.'

Something tightened in his jaw and a guarded sheen hardened his gaze. 'You didn't have to say it. You were ripping my clothes off, and if it hadn't been for that phone call you'd be onto your second or third orgasm by now.'

Argh! How dare he remind her how many times he could make her come? She affected a scornful laugh. 'You think? I would have had to fake it because I do not want you, Vinn. Do you hear me? I. Do. Not. Want. You.'

He stripped off the rest of his clothes and stepped into the bath, sending a miniature tsunami over her body. 'How many times do you reckon you'll have to say it so you actually believe it, hmm?' There was a dangerously silky edge to his tone and he moved up close, capturing her chin between his finger and thumb.

Ailsa tried to brush off his hold like she was swatting an annoying insect. 'Stop touching me.'

His other hand slipped back under the curtain of her hair and he nudged his nose against hers in a playful bump that made her self-control fall over like a house of cards in a hurricane. 'You want me so bad you're shaking with it.'

'I'm shaking with anger and if you don't get your hands off me this instant I'll show you just how angry,' Ailsa said through gritted teeth.

He gave a deep chuckle and slowly but surely coiled a strand of her damp hair around one of his fingers, inexorably tethering her to him. 'I've missed your temper, *cara*. No one does angry quite as sexily as you. It turns me on.'

His pelvis was close enough for her to feel it—the swollen ridge of his arousal calling out to her feminine core like a primal drumbeat, sending an echo through her blood and through her body. 'No one makes me as angry as you do,' Ailsa said. 'I hate you for it. I hate you period.'

'You don't hate me, *cara*.' He slowly unwound her hair from around his finger. 'If you hated me you wouldn't have come home with me from the hospital yesterday.'

Ailsa wrenched out of his hold with a strength she hadn't known she possessed, sending a wave of bathwater over the edge of the tub. 'I didn't have a flipping choice. You brought me there instead of to a hotel as I requested. It was basically abduction, that's what it was. Then you stole my passport and—'

'You know what your trouble is, *cara*? You don't trust yourself around me. That's why you have to paint me as the bad guy because you can't bear the thought that you're the one with the issue.'

How typical of him to make it seem as if *she* was the problem. It was her self-control that was the problem but that was beside the point. 'You think I can't resist you? Think again. I can and I will.' Dangerous words since his hairy legs were currently nudging hers under the soapy water and everything that was female in her was getting hot and bothered.

His smile was confident. I'll-have-you-eating-those-words-in-no-time confident. 'Come here.'

Ailsa sent him a look that would have withered a cactus. 'Dream on, buddy. The days when you could crook your little finger and I would come running are well and truly over.'

He laughed and moved closer, trailing a fingertip down between her soap-covered breasts. 'Then maybe I'll have to come to you, hmm?'

She suppressed a whimper of pleasure as

his finger found her nipple beneath the bubbles. *Why wasn't she moving away?* The slow glide of his finger undid every vertebra on her spine. Only he knew how to dismantle her defences. She could feel her body moistening in preparation, the signal of high arousal. The ache intensified, the need dragging at her, clawing at her, making her desperate in a way that threatened her pride as it had never been threatened before. She tried to think of a way out of the tight corner Vinn had backed her into. How could she satisfy him—*bad choice of word*—without compromising herself? Was there a way she could get Isaac that sponsorship without committing to three months of living with Vinn? 'What if we negotiated the time frame a little?' she said. 'What if I stayed for a week instead of—?'

'One month.'

She gave herself a mental high five. The old Vinn would never negotiate over anything. There was hope after all. 'I was thinking in days rather than—'

He shook his head and sent his finger down her breastbone. 'No deal. One month or nothing. I realise three months is a little long to be away from your business but a month is hardly more than a holiday. And, from what I've heard from Isaac, you haven't had one of those in a while.'

Like you can talk, Mr Workaholic. Ailsa chewed the side of her mouth. One month was better than three and she could catch up on all her Italian clients, giving them the attention they deserved instead of fitting them around her other work. Besides, Vinn's villa was huge. Surely she could keep her distance from him in a house that size? It was a win-win. Well, sort of... 'What have you told Isaac about this...arrangement?'

'I told him the sponsorship would ultimately be up to you.'

Ailsa frowned. 'You told him you were effectively blackmailing me back into your bed?'

'No. I simply told him it was your decision whether I went ahead with the sponsorship.'

'So he'll blame *me* if it doesn't go ahead?'

He gave her an on-off smile that didn't involve his teeth. 'It would be a pity to disappoint him, *sì*?'

Ailsa couldn't refuse. She had no room to refuse. If she refused, her relationship with her brother would end up like her relationship with her mother and stepfather. Damaged. Maybe even destroyed. Isaac would blame her for ever for not being able to follow his dream. It would be *her* fault. Vinn had cleverly orchestrated it so she had no choice but to agree. 'Okay. It's a deal.' She lifted her chin to a combative height. 'But I'm absolutely not sleeping with you.'

His eyes strayed to her mouth as if he couldn't stop himself. 'Who said anything about sleeping?' And then his mouth came crashing down on hers.

It was a kiss she had no way of resisting. No amount of self-control, no amount of anger, no amount of anything was going to be a match for the desire she felt for him. As soon as his lips met hers she was swept up in a maelstrom of lust that threatened to boil the water they were in.

Vinn's hands went to her breasts in a possessive movement that thrilled her as much as it annoyed her. How dare he think she was his for the asking? Not that he'd asked. He'd assumed and he'd assumed right, which was even more annoying. Why did she have no willpower when it came to this man? Why him? What was it about him that made her so weak and needy?

His mouth left hers to suckle on her breasts in a way that lifted every hair on her scalp and sent shivers skating down her spine. No one knew her breasts like he did. No one handled them with such exquisite care and attention. He cradled them as if they were precious and tender, his touch evoking a fevered response from her that had her gasping and mewling like a wanton. His tongue circled her right nipple, rolling and grazing and teasing until she was mindless and limbless. Then he used his teeth in a gentle bite that made an arrow of lust shoot straight to her core. A possessive, you-are-mine-and-only-mine-bite that made her throw herself on his body, desperate for the release only he could give.

His fingers found her folds and within seconds she was flying, careening like an out of control vehicle, her gasps and cries so loud she was almost ashamed of them. She bit down on his shoulder to block the traitorous sound, vaguely satisfied when he grunted and winced. She wanted him to feel pain. Why should it be just her who suffered for this crazy out of control need?

But within moments that was exactly what he seemed to want, for as soon as her stormy, tumultuous orgasm was over he withdrew and sat back against the edge of the bathtub, his arms draped either side, with a cat-standing-beside-an-empty-canary's-cage smile. 'Good?'

Ailsa glanced at the soapy water surrounding his groin that barely concealed his erection. 'Aren't you going to—?'

'Not right now.' He vaulted out of the bathtub in one effortless movement and reached for one of the fluffy white towels and began roughly drying himself.

Ailsa silently seethed at the way he was demonstrating his superior self-control. He'd made her come but he wasn't going to indulge his own pleasure just to show how he could resist her. *Damn it.* She would show him how hard it was to resist her. She got out of the bath and began drying herself with one of the towels, not roughly as he had done but with slow sensual strokes. She put one foot on the edge of the bath and leaned over to dry between her toes, feeling his eyes devour her derrière. She changed feet and swung her wet hair behind one shoulder and leaned forward again. He was the only man she had ever felt completely comfortable with being naked. She had the same hang-ups most women did about their bodies, but Vinn had always made her feel like a goddess.

She put her foot back down to the floor and turned to face him. 'Would you pass me that body moisturiser over there?'

He picked up a bottle of luxurious honey-suckle-scented creamy lotion. 'This one?'

Ailsa took it from him with a coy smile. 'Want me to rub your back for you?'

His eyes darkened with simmering lust. 'You're playing a dangerous game, *cara*.'

Ailsa squirted some lotion into one of her hands and then put the bottle aside to emulsify the lotion between her hands before smoothing some over her breasts. 'It's really important to moisturise after a hot bath. It keeps your skin supple and smooth.'

His eyes watched every movement of her hands moving over her breasts, the tension in the air at snapping point. When she reached for the bottle of lotion again his hand was already on it. He held her gaze while he poured some out into the middle of his palm. 'Turn around.'

Ailsa turned and shivered when his hand began a slow, sensual stroking motion from the tops of her shoulders to the base of her spine and then even further into the cleavage of her buttocks. Her body clenched tight with need, the sexy glide of his hands in the intimate spaces of her flesh making her forget everything but the desire that throbbed with every single beat of her pulse. He moved his hands to the front of her body, stroking over her breasts and down over her stomach before going lower. She could feel the brush of his body from behind, the hard ridge of his erection against her bottom making her need for him escalating to the point of pain.

He turned her in his arms and looked at her through sexily hooded eyes. 'You know I want you.'

Ailsa moved closer so the jut of his erection was pushed against her belly. 'Make love to me, Vinn.'

He framed her face in his hands, his eyes holding hers. 'That wasn't what you were saying a few minutes ago.'

'I'm saying it now.'

His eyes dipped to her mouth, lingering there for a pulsing moment. Then his mouth came down and covered hers in a searing kiss that inflamed her need like petrol on a fire.

He held her body closer, the glide of naked flesh against naked flesh stirring her senses into rapture. Ailsa linked her arms around his neck, stepping on tiptoe so she could feel the proud bulge of his arousal close to where she throbbed the most.

Vinn deepened the kiss, tangling his tongue with hers, making her whimper at the back of her throat. With his mouth still clamped to hers, they moved almost blindly to the bedroom where he laid her down on the bed and came down over her, propping his weight on his forearms with his legs in a sexy tangle with hers.

He lifted his mouth off hers, looking at her with a direct and probing gaze. 'Are you sure about this?'

Ailsa had never felt surer of anything. She would think about the implications of making love with Vinn again later. For now all she could think of was how wonderful it felt to be pinned to the bed with his weight, with his engorged length thick and heavy between her thighs. She traced a fingertip over his bottom lip, her stomach tilting when she encountered his prickly stubble just below. 'I want you. I don't want to want you, but I can't seem to help it.'

He pressed a brief hard kiss to her mouth. 'I feel the same.'

Ailsa moved beneath him, opening her legs to accommodate him, breathing in a quick sharp breath when he entered her swiftly and smoothly. Her body gripped him, welcoming him back with a tight clench of greedy muscles. He began a torturously slow rhythm but she egged him on by clutching him by the buttocks and bringing him closer with each slick thrust. She could feel the pressure building, the tension in her core so intense but unable to finally let go without that extra bit of friction. He slipped a hand between their bodies, finding the swollen heart of her and caressing it with just the right amount of pressure to send her flying over the edge.

The orgasm smashed into her, rolling her over and over and over, sending waves and currents and eddies of pleasure through her body. It was almost too much and she tried to shrink back from it but Vinn wouldn't allow her to do so and kept on caressing her until she was in the middle of another orgasm, even more powerful than the first. She gasped and cried out as the storm broke over her, tossing her every which way like a shaken rag doll.

She gained enough consciousness to feel Vinn pump his way through his own powerful orgasm, his guttural groan thrilling her because it made her feel wanted and needed and desired. She knew she could have been anybody, but he hadn't chosen anybody.

He had chosen her.

He hadn't made love with anyone since she'd left. It didn't mean he loved her. It meant he wanted to draw a line under their relationship once it was finally over, but she didn't want to think about that now. She closed her eyes and sighed as his arms gathered her close, just like the old days when she'd fooled herself this was a normal relationship with no secrets and hidden agendas.

Vinn stroked a hand down her thigh. 'I would have used a condom but since neither of us has been with anyone else I thought it'd be okay. I assume you've still got your contraceptive implant?'

Ailsa's stomach pitched. Her implant had been up for renewal a couple of months ago but she'd put off making an appointment with her doctor. Why had she left it so late to get it changed? She knew exactly why—because she hadn't had sex with anyone.

Because she hadn't been able to even *think* about having sex with anyone other than Vinn.

Would the device still be working? She hoped and prayed…and yet a tiny part of her couldn't help thinking about a baby that looked exactly like Vinn. *No. No. No.* She mustn't think about it. *Must not. Must not. Must not think about it.* Allowing those thoughts into her head made it harder to ignore them the next time.

And there would be a next time.

There had been a lot of them lately. Thoughts. Treacherous thoughts of holding a baby in her arms. She was nearly thirty years old. Her mother had given birth to her at eighteen and to Isaac at twenty-eight. But how could Ailsa think of being a mother to a child?

She pushed those thoughts away and gave Vinn a you-know-me-so-well smile. 'Yep. I sure do.'

He traced a slow circle around her belly button. 'You're the only person I've ever made love to without a condom.'

'Because we were married, right?'

'Not just that…' His eyes went to her mouth for a moment before coming back to her gaze. 'I never felt any other relationship had the potential to work as ours did.'

Ailsa lowered her gaze to concentrate on the dark stubble on his chin. 'It would only have worked if I'd caved in to every one of your commands. I wasn't prepared to do that. I'm still not.'

He brushed the hair back from her forehead with a wistful look on his face. 'Maybe you're right. We should have had a fling and left it at that.'

Ailsa tiptoed her fingertip down from his sternum to his belly button. 'Changed your mind about that back rub?'

His eyes glinted. 'You've talked me into it.' And then his mouth came down and covered hers.

CHAPTER SIX

WHEN AILSA WOKE the next morning back at the villa there was no sign of Vinn. Well, apart from the indentation of his head on the pillow beside her and the little twinges in her intimate muscles, that was. He had taken her back to the villa late last night rather than spending the whole night at the hotel, and made love to her all over again. It made her wonder how she had gone so long without him making love to her. It made her wonder how she would cope once their 'reconciliation' was over.

She had a refreshing shower and, wrapping herself in a fluffy white bath towel, looked balefully at her creased clothes from the day before. There was any number of outfits in the walk-in wardrobe but somehow stepping back into the role of trophy wife—temporary as it was—was a little off-putting. Was she losing herself all over again? Capitulating to Vinn's demands as if she had no will and mind of her own?

But this was about his grandfather more than about her and Vinn. Dom was the one they were doing this for. She was still trying to make up her mind what to do about her clothes when her phone rang from her handbag on the end of the bed. She took it out and saw it was a call from her brother. 'Hi Isaac.'

'Vinn told me you're okay with him sponsoring me,' Isaac said with such excitement in his voice it soothed some of her residual anger at Vinn. Some. Not all. 'I don't know how to thank you. I thought you'd be all dog-in-the-manger about it but he said you were amazing about it. Really amazing.'

'What else did he say about me?'

There was a little silence.

'He said you two were working on a reconciliation. Is it true? Are you back together?'

Ailsa hated lying to her brother but couldn't see any way out of it. If Isaac knew what was really going on he might refuse Vinn's sponsorship. She couldn't allow Isaac's one chance to hit the big time to be overshadowed by how Vinn had orchestrated things. 'It's true but it's only a trial reconciliation. Things might not work out so don't get your hopes up.'

'I'm happy for you, Ailsa. Really happy because you haven't been happy since you left him.'

'You don't have to worry about me, kiddo,' Ailsa said. 'I'm a big girl who can take care of herself.'

'What actually broke you guys up? You've always changed the subject when anyone mentions—'

'I'd rather not talk about it if you don't mind—'

'He didn't cheat on you, did he? I know he was a bit of a playboy before he met you but he wouldn't have married you if he didn't want to settle down.'

Ailsa let out a short sigh. 'No. He didn't cheat on me. We just…disagreed on stuff.'

'Like having kids?'

She was a little shocked at the direct way her brother was speaking. She had never overtly discussed her decision not to have children with him or with her mother and stepfather. It was something she didn't like discussing because it reminded her of why she'd made the decision in the first place. They knew her career was her top priority and she allowed them to think that was her main reason. Her only reason. 'Why would you say that?'

'I just wondered if you've been put off the idea of having kids because of Mum and Dad breaking up.'

Alisa knew the divorce had hit Isaac harder than it had her. She had moved out of home soon after but he had still been at school and had to move between two households for access visits. Their parents had done their best to keep things civil, but Ailsa knew there were times when things had been a little messy emotionally. 'Lots of people come from broken homes these days,' she said, skirting around the issue. 'It's the new normal.'

'So you do want kids?'

'For God's sake, Isaac.' Ailsa laughed but, to her chagrin, it sounded a little fake. 'I'm only twenty-nine. There's still plenty of time yet to decide if I want to go down that track.'

'Remember when you gave away all your childhood toys a few years back? All your dolls and stuff? I wondered why you would do that if you planned to have kids of your own some day.'

'I was doing a clean-up,' Ailsa said. 'All that

stuff was taking up too much space at Mum's place after the divorce.'

'That wasn't the only thing,' Isaac said. 'You used to go all goochy-goochy-goo and embarrassing when you saw someone with a pram. Now you look the other way.'

No wonder her brother was an ace golfer. He had eyesight like an eagle's. 'Not every woman is cut out to be a mother. I have my career in any case and—'

'But you'd be a great mum, Ails.' He used his pet name for her, the name he had called her when he'd been too young to pronounce her name properly—except back then he'd had an adorable lisp. 'Sometimes I think you've been better at it than Mum. She's never been all that maternal, especially with you.'

'It's not going to happen,' Ailsa said. 'And certainly not with Vinn.'

'Oh… I didn't realise there were problems. But you can have IVF. It's not like Vinn couldn't afford it.'

'I do not need IVF.' And she could almost guarantee nor did Vinn. 'It's a choice I've made and I would appreciate it if everyone would damn well accept it.'

'Sorry. I didn't mean to upset you. I just

wanted to call and say thanks for agreeing to the sponsorship. You have no idea what this means to me. I wouldn't be able to get anywhere near the pro circuit without Vinn's help. Three years all expenses paid. It's a dream offer.'

Ailsa wished she hadn't sounded so…so defensive. 'I'm sorry for biting your head off. I'm just feeling a little emotional right now. Vinn's grandfather is still in ICU and it's—'

'Yeah, he told me about that. It's kind of cool you're there with him, supporting him through such a tough time.'

I'm not here by choice. The words were on the tip of her tongue but she didn't say them out loud. Besides, she had made a choice. She had chosen to accept Vinn's deal and now she had to lie on the bed she had made.

Her only consolation was Vinn had joined her in it.

Vinn had left Ailsa to sleep in because he didn't trust himself not to reach for her again. And again and again and again. The need she awakened in him was ferocious. Ferocious and greedy and out of control, and the one thing he needed right now was to be in control. They could have a one-month fling. It would serve two purposes: get his grandfather through the danger period and draw a final line under Vinn's relationship with Ailsa.

He'd phoned the hospital first thing and the ICU specialist had informed him his grandfather was still stable. It was good news but he didn't feel he could relax until his grandfather was off the ventilator and conscious again and truly out of danger.

Vinn knew Ailsa had only slept with him to prove a point—to prove he couldn't resist her. Which was pretty much true. He couldn't. But in time he would be able to. He would make sure of it. He would have to because their relationship had a time limit on it and he was adamant about enforcing it. He would have liked three months with her because three months would have given his grandfather ample time to recuperate. But he'd agreed to the compromise because three months was a long time for her to be away from her business. In the two years since she'd left him she had built up a successful interior decorating business that had enormous potential for expansion. It was a little unsettling to think she had only achieved that success once she'd left him. He hadn't intended to hold her back career-wise but she had seemed unhappy and unfulfilled in her previous job and he'd thought she would jump at the chance of being his wife, with all the benefits the position entailed.

Their affair had been so intense and passionate and he hadn't wanted to lose her…or at least not like that. He'd thought an offer of marriage would demonstrate his commitment even if he hadn't been in love with her. He had never been in love with anyone. He wasn't sure he had the falling in love gene. Maybe he was more like his father than he realised.

Although, unlike his father, he devoted himself to his work, to the business he had saved and rebuilt out of the ashes his father had left. He was proud of what he had achieved. It had taken guts and sacrifice and discipline to bring it back from the brink but he had done it. He'd owed it to his grandfather to restore the family business built over generations, to undo the damage his father had inflicted. He had built up the Gagliardi name to be something to be proud of again, instead of something of which to be ashamed.

But making love with Ailsa again reminded him of all the reasons why he'd wanted her in the first place. Would a month be enough to get her out of his system? Or would it only feed the fire still smouldering deep inside him that he had relentlessly, ruthlessly tried to smother with work?

Ailsa came downstairs but was a little miffed to find Vinn had left the villa without speaking to her first. There was a note left on the kitchen bench informing her he had gone to visit his grandfather. Surely he could have walked upstairs to deliver the message in person? Why hadn't he? And why hadn't he taken her with him to the hospital? Wouldn't his grandfather be expecting her to be by Vinn's side? But then she recalled Vinn telling her his grandfather was being kept on a ventilator for a few days until he recovered from the surgery. It appeased her slightly, but still it was a chilling reminder of the charade they were playing. He would only want her 'on task' when his grandfather was awake and conscious.

And, of course, when Vinn had her in his bed. She was annoyed with herself for making love with him so soon. *Damn it.* Why hadn't she kept her distance? It was as if he had the upper hand again. He knew how much she wanted him. He wanted her too, which was some minor consolation, but she would be a fool to think he would always want her. Once their divorce was final he would move on. He would not spend weeks, months, almost two years remembering and missing and aching for every touch, every kiss, every passionate encounter. He wouldn't be curled up lonely in bed, wishing she were back in his arms. He would find someone else to have his babies for him and would not give her another thought, while she would be left with her memories of him and her regrets over what she wanted but couldn't have.

Ailsa had finished making some calls to her assistant Brooke in her studio back in London when she heard the front door of the villa open. But the footsteps sounded nothing like Vinn's firm purposeful stride. She poked her head around the sitting room door to see the elderly housekeeper Carlotta shuffling in carrying some shopping.

'So you're back.' The old woman's tone could hardly be described as welcoming but Ailsa refused to be intimidated.

'Can I help you with those bags?'

Carlotta grudgingly allowed Ailsa to take the bags and carry them to the kitchen. Ailsa placed them on the bench and began unpacking them. 'Why are you here today? Vinn told me you had this week off.'

'How long are you staying?' The housekeeper's gaze was as sharp as her voice.

Ailsa shifted her lips from side to side, wondering if she should try a different tack with Vinn's housekeeper. In the past she had been quick to bite out of hurt, but she wondered now if that had been the wrong approach. 'I'm only staying a month. I presume Vinn told you his plan to keep me here until Dom is out of danger?'

Carlotta made a sound like a snort and glanced at the rings on Ailsa's hand. 'Long enough for you to get your hands on more expensive jewellery, no doubt. I'm surprised you didn't pawn those when you had the chance.'

Ailsa reined in her temper with an effort. 'I didn't take them with me. I left them in Vinn's bedside drawer. I left everything he gave me behind—but surely you know that?'

Carlotta's expression flickered with puzzlement for a moment but then her features came back to her default position of haughty disapproval. 'Why are you back now if not for money? How much is he paying you?'

Ailsa could feel her cheeks giving her away. 'It's not about the money... It's about Dom's health and my brother's—'

'It was always about the money,' Carlotta said. 'You didn't love him. You've never loved Vinn. You just wanted to be married to a rich and powerful man to bolster your self-esteem.'

Ailsa bit the inside of her mouth to stop herself flinging back a retort. But, in a way, Carlotta had hit the nail on the head with startling accuracy. She had married Vinn for the wrong reasons. She had so wanted to be normal and acceptable, and what better way to prove it than to marry a man everyone looked up to and admired for his drive and focus and wealth? It had certainly helped that she'd found him irresistibly attractive. But she had grown to love him over the short time they were married, which was why she'd been so terrified when he'd brought up the topic of having a family.

How could *she* give him what he most wanted?

'If you cared about him you would have come back when his father died,' Carlotta said.

'I didn't know his father had died until he told me about it the day before yesterday.' Had it only been two days? It shamed Ailsa to think Vinn had managed to lure her back into his bed in little more than forty-eight hours. Had she so little willpower? So little self-respect?

Carlotta gave her a disbelieving look and then made a business of unloading the shopping out of the bags. 'He wasn't close to his father but it brought back a lot of memories for him about when his mother died. And where was his wife when all this was going on? Living it up in London with not even the decency to call him or send a card and flowers.'

Ailsa decided to ignore the dig at her supposed lack of decency in order to pursue the subject of Vinn's mother's death and the impact it had on him. She'd tried to get him to talk about it but he'd always resisted. Should she try again? 'I didn't realise you were close to Vinn's mother. What was she like?'

Carlotta's expression lost some of its tightness. 'She was a wonderful person. Warm and friendly and loving and she loved Vinn so much. Motherhood suited her. Vinn was what she lived for. She should never have married Vinn's father but he was a charming suitor and she was shy and got swept off her feet before she realised what he was truly like.' She gave a heartfelt sigh and folded one of the shopping bags into a neat square. 'Vinn took her death hard, but then what four-year-old wouldn't? He used to be such a happy out-going child but after his mother was taken from him he changed. Became more serious and hardly ever smiled. It was like he grew up overnight.'

'Her death must have hit you hard too,' Ailsa said.

Carlotta gave a sad twist of her mouth. 'I worked for her as a housekeeper but we became friends. When Vinn moved in with his grandparents I came too. I've worked on and off for the Gagliardi family for most of my life. In some ways they *are* my family.'

'I can see now why you only wanted the best for Vinn,' Ailsa said, toying with an imaginary crumb on the kitchen bench. 'No wonder you didn't accept me.'

The elderly housekeeper looked at her for a long moment. 'I would have accepted you if I'd thought you loved him.'

'We didn't have that type of relationship,' Ailsa said. 'I know it's hard for you to understand but he didn't love me either so—'

'So you didn't have the courage to love him regardless.' The barb of disapproval was back in the old woman's tone.

Was loving Vinn a courageous or a crazy thing to do? Lusting after him was madness enough. Loving him would be emotional suicide because even if by some remote chance he grew to love her, what would he think of her once he found out she was the child of a ghastly criminal?

After spending the rest of the day reflecting on her conversation with Carlotta, Ailsa decided more could be served by drawing Vinn out about his childhood. She needed to try harder to understand him, to get to know the man he was behind the successful businessman. But she couldn't do that if she was constantly falling into bed with him. Making love with him within forty-eight hours of seeing him after a twenty-two month separation was a pathetic indictment on her part. How had she succumbed so quickly? So readily? Why couldn't she have gone ahead with the charade without sleeping with him, as he'd first proposed?

Like that was ever going to work.

She had to get a grip on her self-control. Sex with Vinn was delightfully distracting but she needed to get to know him better. What motivated him to work so hard? What had made him marry a woman he didn't love when he could have had anyone? What was it about her that made him make such a commitment without love as the motivation?

She knew the more she slept with him the harder it would be to leave when the month was up. She had to keep reminding herself she was in the process of divorcing him. This was not a fairy tale where the handsome prince came riding back into town to claim his princess bride. This was a fake reconciliation in order to reduce the stress on an elderly man during a medical crisis.

Ailsa moved some of her clothes out of the walk-in wardrobe and into the bedroom she'd used the first night, further down the corridor from Vinn's. She was resetting her boundaries, making sure he got the message she wasn't the pushover he thought she was. Did he really think ten million pounds would buy her back into his bed? She'd scratched the itch and now the itch would have to go away. Or if it didn't she would damn well ignore it because it was time she made it absolutely clear to him that he didn't have the same hold over her as he had in the past. If they were going to sleep together then they would have to talk as well. Use not just their bodies but also their minds. To connect in the way they should have done in the first place.

Ailsa came out of the en suite bathroom of the spare bedroom to find Vinn waiting for her.

'Why have you moved your things in here?' He waved a hand towards the pile of clothes on the bed she hadn't yet put away.

She tightened the towel she was wearing around her body. 'Because I think it's best if we keep things on a platonic basis for now.'

'Platonic?' The mockery in his tone was as jarring as the raking look he gave her towel-clad body. 'A bit late for that, don't you think?'

'I shouldn't have slept with you. You caught me in a weak moment. It won't be repeated. We need to talk to each other instead of having sex. Really talk.'

He came to stand in front of her. 'Such a

stubborn little thing.' He stroked the upper curves of her breasts showing above the towel. 'You want me and yet you deny yourself because you think it will give me an edge.'

Ailsa wasn't too happy about being so transparent. 'The trouble with you, Vinn, is you're not used to someone saying no to you.'

He smiled a lazy smile and sent his finger on another slow journey, this time to her cleavage, dipping his finger into the space between her breasts. 'You say no with your words but your body says an emphatic yes.'

Ailsa trembled under his touch, the leisurely movement of his finger against the sensitive flesh of her breasts making her nipples tighten and ripples of pleasure flow through the rest of her body. Before she'd met Vinn, her breasts were just breasts. Things that had sprouted on her chest when she was thirteen. Things she put in her bra and checked once a month for lumps. But since his hands and mouth had explored and tasted and tantalised them, she couldn't even look at her breasts without thinking about his dark head bent over them and his wickedly clever lips and tongue and teeth, and the sensual havoc they could do to her.

She glanced at his tanned finger against the creamy whiteness of her cleavage, her breath stalling in her throat and rampant need spiralling through her body. How could her body betray her like this? How could it be so needy and hungry and greedy for his touch? He slid his finger deeper into the valley of her cleavage. Well, *valley* was probably a bit of an exaggeration. But, even though her breasts were on the small side, that had never seemed to matter to Vinn. He made her feel as if she could have been a lingerie model. 'Vinn... I...'

'Don't talk, *cara*.' He brought his mouth to the edge of hers, playing with her lips with his in a teasing come-and-play-with-me nudge. 'Just feel.'

Ailsa was pretty much incapable of speech. Saying no or pretending she didn't want him seemed pointless when her body was on fire and red-hot need was clawing at her insides with rapacious hunger. Had she ever been able to say no to Vinn? 'I'm going to hate myself for this tomorrow,' she said and bumped her lips against his.

'It's just sex.' He gave her lips another nudge

and then followed it up with a bone-melting sweep of his tongue.

Ailsa glanced up into his eyes. 'Is it just sex?'

'What else could it be?' His mouth did another teasing movement against hers, making any thought of resisting him move even further out of her reach.

She braced herself against the surge of lust roaring through her body by placing one of her hands flat against his chest, the other somehow holding her towel in place. 'But why now? It seems so…so out of the blue. We've had zero contact other than through our lawyers for almost two years.'

His stubble grazed her cheek as he shifted position to go back to just below her ear. 'Because I've missed you.'

Ailsa shivered when his tongue found the shell of her ear. *He'd missed her?* Her old friend sarcasm came on duty before any romantic notions could take a foothold. She eased back a little to look at him eye to eye. 'But you knew where I was. There was nothing to stop you coming to see me in London. You didn't even call me or send a text. The only communication I got was through your lawyer a month later, once I'd instigated the divorce.'

His expression became rueful and his hands fell away from her body. He put some distance between them and then he rubbed one of his hands over the back of his neck as if trying to release a knot of tension. 'I had planned to come and see you but then I got caught up with—'

'Work has always been your first priority, hasn't it? And yet you won't allow it to be mine.'

His hand dropped back by his side and his mouth took on a grim line. 'My father died two days after you left.'

Ailsa was shocked into silence. She'd been under the impression Vinn's father had died a few months ago, not within two days of her leaving. She tried to think back to her conversation with Carlotta. Had the housekeeper said when Vinn's father had died? Was that why Carlotta was so convinced Ailsa didn't care about him? Had he been going to contact her and then got caught up in the tragedy of burying his father? When she hadn't heard from him after a week she'd instigated the divorce proceedings with her lawyer, figuring Vinn had had plenty of time to say what needed to be said. She'd taken his silence as his answer and yet now she realised there had been a good reason for that silence.

Remorse, regret, shame at her impetuosity rained down on her like stinging hail. Why hadn't she waited a few more days? Why hadn't *she* contacted him? Pride. Stubborn mulish pride had kept her in London with her phone mostly turned off because she'd wanted him to sweat it out. To miss her. To feel threatened he might lose her.

But *she* had lost him...

Vinn released a rough-edged breath. 'I probably should've contacted you to at least tell you he'd passed away but it was such a hideous time, with that poor family he'd nearly wiped out and his grieving girlfriend's family... I don't know...' He sighed again. 'I just had to get through each day. There wasn't time to think about my own stuff with the police and coroner's investigation and the distraught relatives threatening legal action, not to mention the constant press attention. And then, when I got your lawyer's letter informing me you were demanding a divorce, I figured it was too late to change your mind.'

It hadn't been too late. Ailsa swallowed the words behind a wall of regret. If only she had waited a few more days. A week or two…even a month. Why had she been so insistent on drawing that line in the sand so firmly it cut her off from him completely? But what was the point in admitting how immature and foolish she'd been? Their relationship was beyond salvage because they wanted different things out of life.

'I had no idea your father died so soon after I left… I'm so sorry. It must have been an awful time for you and Dom. I didn't see anything in the press back in London, otherwise I would have—'

'What? Sent flowers?' A note of sarcasm entered his voice. 'Just think—you could've sent two for the price of one. A wreath for my father and another one for the death of our marriage.'

For once, Ailsa refrained from flinging back an equally sarcastic response. She realised, shamefully for the first time, that he used sarcasm as she did. As a shield to keep people from discovering the truth about his emotional state. He might not have been close to his father, but a parent's death was still a huge event in one's life. Sometimes the death of a difficult parent was even trickier to deal with because of the ambiguity of feelings, and the nagging regret that those issues couldn't be resolved once death had placed its final stamp on things.

'I'm really sorry you had such a horrible time dealing with your dad's death and all the other stuff so soon after we...split up. But maybe if you'd contacted me straight away to tell me about your father's accident—'

'You would have come crawling back?' The dark light in his eyes warned her she was flirting with danger. 'You are assuming, of course, that I would've taken you back.'

Ailsa straightened her spine and forced herself to hold his gaze. 'I wouldn't have come back unless you apologised first for being such an arrogant chauvinist.'

'I see no need to apologise for wanting what most people want, and if you're honest with yourself you want it too. You're allowing your parents' divorce to dictate your life. That's crazy. And childish.'

'It's not about my parents' divorce,' Ailsa said. 'Why is it so hard for you to understand I don't want children? When a man says he doesn't want kids no one says anything. But when a woman does, everyone takes it upon themselves to talk her out of her decision as if she's being impossibly selfish.'

'Okay, so if it's not about your parents' divorce then what is it about?' His gaze was so direct she felt like a bug on a corkboard.

'I just told you.'

'You told me you didn't want children, but is it just about the interruption to your career?'

Ailsa shifted her gaze and made a business of securing the towel around her body. 'I'm not maternal. I never have been. My career is the most important thing to me.'

'Isaac once told me you were more of a mother to him than your mother was,' Vinn said. 'He said in many ways you still are.'

Ailsa wondered exactly how chummy her brother and Vinn were these days. But then she realised Isaac had always idolised Vinn from the moment she'd introduced them to each other. Vinn talked to her brother man to man, not man to child or even man to teenager. But how much of their childhood had Isaac shared with him?

'I'm ten years older than Isaac. I was just being a big sister. Mum did her best, but she found being a mother hard, with me especially, but with Isaac too.'

His frown brought his eyebrows together. 'Why you especially?'

Ailsa wished she'd kept her mouth shut but for some strange reason it was becoming more and more tempting to tell him about her background. When she'd first met him she hadn't wanted him to see her as anything other than a normal young woman. As the normal young woman she had been until the age of fifteen when she'd stumbled across the ugly truth. She didn't want to be a freak. She didn't want to be the outcome of a hideous crime. She wanted to be normal. 'I was a difficult, fractious baby who refused to take the breast and slept fitfully. She had trouble bonding with me. And she was young—only eighteen when she had me so it was hard for her.'

'But she still loved you and wanted you.'

She met his frowning gaze. Could she risk telling him the whole truth or would it be safer to give him a cut-down version of it? She was tired of holding this dark secret inside.

Tired and lonely and utterly isolated.

No one but her mother and stepfather knew about the circumstances of her birth but they didn't like talking about it any more than she did. The lie was the elephant in the room quietly rotting in the corner. Wasn't it time to tell Vinn? He'd been her husband, her lover, and in some ways the first person who'd made her feel normal and acceptable. Then there would be one other person she could talk to about the shame that clung to her like grime. It wouldn't change the circumstances of her conception but it would mean she didn't have to keep it a secret from him any longer. It was too late to repair their marriage, mostly because they shouldn't have married in the first place, but surely she owed him the truth before the divorce was made final? 'She didn't want me, Vinn. That was the problem. She never wanted me.'

'Why do you say that? Surely she didn't say that to you?'

Ailsa gave him a tortured smile. 'Some things you don't have to say out loud, especially to kids. I was a mistake. I should never have been born.'

Vinn's expression was full of concern and he came up close to rest his hands on the top of her bare shoulders, his long tanned fingers warm and gentle on her flesh. 'But what about your dad, Michael? Does he make you feel the same as your mother?'

Ailsa knew she had come to a crossroads in her relationship with Vinn. If she took the truth turn, things would never be the same. If she took the white lie turn, things would be the same but different. It was strange because she was dressed in nothing but a fluffy white bath towel and it felt as if the towel symbolised the white lie she was hiding behind. Once she stripped it away she would be naked.

Emotionally naked.

Vinn's hands gave her shoulders an encouraging squeeze. 'Talk to me, *cara*.' His voice was deep and gravelly, making her insides melt.

Ironic he should say that when she'd been the one to insist he talk to her. 'Vinn…' Ailsa sighed and placed her hands on his chest and suppressed a shiver as she felt his warm hard muscles flex beneath her palms, as if her touch shook him to the core as his did to her. 'The thing is… Michael isn't really my father. He's my stepfather.' She took a deep breath and went on. 'I have never met my real father and nor would I ever want to.'

'Why's that?' There was a note of unease

in Vinn's tone and a gentling in the way his hands held her.

Ailsa swallowed tightly. 'My mother was raped at a party. She didn't tell anyone about the assault as she blamed herself for getting tipsy. By the time she realised she was pregnant it was too late to do anything about it. She eventually told my stepfather, who was her boyfriend at the time, and he insisted on marrying her and bringing me up as his own.'

Vinn's face was riven with shock but overlying that was concern—rich, dark concern that pulsed in his gaze as it held hers. 'Oh, *cara*... That's so... I don't know what to say. When did you find out? Was it recently? Did they tell you or—?'

'I found out when I was fifteen. They were never going to tell me. They'd made a pact about it.'

A heavy frown carved deep into his forehead. 'You've known since you were *fifteen*?'

Ailsa tried not to be daunted by the slightly accusatory tone of his voice. 'I overheard them arguing about it one day when I came home earlier than expected. My stepfather thought I should be told but Mum didn't. I confronted them about it and my mother reluctantly told me about the assault.'

'But Ailsa, why didn't you tell me?' His voice was hoarse and his hands fell away from her as if he couldn't bear to touch her. 'Why keep something like that from me? Your own husband, for God's sake.'

Ailsa tried to read his expression. Was it anger or disgust that made his eyes so dark and glittery? 'So this is suddenly all about you now, is it?' she said. 'I didn't tell you because I didn't want you to look at me like you're looking at me now. As something disgusting and freakish and ghastly.'

'I am not looking at you like—'

'Do you know what it's like to find out you're the child of rape?' Ailsa said, not giving him time to answer. 'It's disgusting and freakish and ghastly. Every time I look in the mirror I'm reminded of it. I look nothing like my mother, and of course I don't look like my stepfather. The face my mother sees when she sees me is the face of her rapist. A man who has never been charged and is probably out there with a wife and kids of his own by now. How could my mother ever love me? I'm the embodiment of her worst nightmare.

She thought she was doing the right thing in keeping me. Michael thought he was doing the right thing by marrying her and bringing me up as his own. But they wouldn't have got married if it hadn't been for me. Their relationship was doomed from the start and it was my fault. No surprise they got a divorce a few months after I found out. I've ruined so many lives.'

'*Cara…*' Vinn took a step towards her, his features still contorted with concern. 'You've done no such thing. You're the innocent victim here. Your mother too, and Michael. What happened was shocking. Even more shocking that justice hasn't been served.'

Ailsa turned away, frightened she might break down in front of him. Over the years she had taught herself not to cry. She vented her distress in other ways—tantrums, anger, sarcasm and put-downs.

She felt him come up behind her, his tall frame like a strong fortress. His hands went to her waist this time, resting there with such exquisite gentleness a ropey knot formed in her throat and she had to swallow furiously a couple of times to clear it.

Vinn rested his chin on the top of her head

and cradled her against his body in a support-ive embrace that stirred her body into fever-ish awareness. 'Thank you for telling me. It must have been difficult for you to keep that to yourself all this time.'

Ailsa slowly turned in his arms and some-how her arms were around his waist as if programmed to do so. The way their bodies fitted together felt so natural, so right, like two pieces of a complicated puzzle slotting together. She looked up into his gaze and was surprised to see tenderness. 'You have to promise me something, Vinn. Please don't tell Isaac.'

His frown was back. 'He doesn't know?'

'No, and I don't want him to, nor do my mother or stepfather want him to find out.'

'Is that wise? I mean…keeping this a secret hasn't helped you or your mother or stepfa-ther. In fact, it's made things so much worse.'

Ailsa dropped her arms from around his waist and stepped away. 'Don't make me re-gret telling you, Vinn. I absolutely insist Isaac doesn't find out. I couldn't bear it if he no longer saw me as his sister. I just couldn't bear it.'

There was a beat or two of silence.

'All right.' His tone was both resigned and reluctant. 'If that's what you insist. But will you tell your mother and Michael I now know?'

Ailsa hadn't thought that far ahead. She chewed at her lower lip, wondering if she'd done the right thing in telling Vinn after all. 'I don't see either of them much these days.' She chanced a glance at him and saw he was frowning again. 'They weren't too happy with me when I announced I was divorcing you. They thought I should've tried harder.'

'I'm the one who should have tried harder, *cara*.' His voice was weighted with regret and his expression rueful.

Ailsa was still thinking of something to say in response when his phone rang from where he'd left it on the bedside table. Vinn moved across to pick it up and, after a brief conversation, the lines of worry etched into his face began to ease. 'Thank you for letting me know. *Ciao*.'

'Was that the hospital?'

Vinn nodded and let out a breath that sounded as if he'd been holding it for years. 'They've removed him from the ventilator. He's conscious and stable for the moment.'

Ailsa let out her own breath she hadn't realised she'd been holding. 'I'm so glad. Do you want to go and see him or is it too early?'

'I'll go in now but you stay here. It's just close relatives allowed at the moment.'

She tried not to feel shut out but how could she not? She wasn't close family any more. Strictly speaking, she was no longer Vinn's wife. She was nothing to him now. Sure, he might desire her but how long would that last? He'd set a time limit on their 'reconciliation'. She was little more than a mistress to him now. Someone to have sex with but not to build a future and a life together.

CHAPTER SEVEN

VINN DROVE LIKE a robot to the hospital to see his grandfather but it was Ailsa on his mind, not the frail old man. How could she have kept the secret of her background from him? Had he known her at all back then? Why had she felt she couldn't tell him something so important about her childhood? It explained so much about her reluctance to discuss having a family. He could only imagine what it must feel like, not knowing who her father was. He knew his all too well and, while deeply ashamed of the things his father had done and having been hurtfully and repeatedly let down by him, Vinn had still loved him.

While on one level he could understand Ailsa keeping her dark secret from him, another part was angry she hadn't trusted him with it earlier. There was a war going on inside him—a war between anger and compassion. One part of him recognised the trauma it must have been for Ailsa to find out her father was a criminal—a beast who'd taken advantage of her mother in the most despicable way. And yet another part of him felt angry Ailsa hadn't opened up to him. It was ironic but they had shared so much sexually, been adventurous and open about what they liked and didn't like. How could she have shared her body so openly and yet not her heart?

Not that he had any right to sit in judgement. He knew there were things he hadn't shared either. Things that had shaped him, moulded him, changed him. Like losing his mother so unexpectedly and the grief and bone-deep sadness that followed—sadness that still clung to him, haunting him with a lingering feeling of isolation and loneliness. He had learned from an early age to be self-sufficient.

To rely on no one but himself.

Even though his grandparents had been as supportive as they could, Vinn had still kept a part of himself contained, held back in case they too were snatched away from him.

Finding out about Ailsa's past now, when they were so close to divorcing, deepened his regret. Made it harder to grapple with because he had always blamed her for the breakup. He had given her everything money could buy, spoilt her as most women loved to be spoilt, but she had given nothing of herself but access to her body.

He felt shut out.

Locked out.

Lied to.

He'd made it his business to know every inch of her body. He had prided himself on their sex life—the frequency of it, the power and potency of it. The monumental satisfaction of it. But she had kept the most important information about herself from him.

It reminded him of how his father had kept the truth about his mother's death from him. But in the end it had only made things worse. He hadn't been adequately prepared for the blunt shock of the truth. He'd always wondered if his father had gently led him through that time with honesty instead of cowardly lies and cover-ups, he might have coped better with the loss of his mother.

Now he was left floundering again. Shocked. Stunned. Angry that Ailsa hadn't trusted him enough with the truth, as painful and heartbreaking as it was. If he had known earlier he might have been able to rescue their relationship, to tread more carefully over the issue of having a family. But he hadn't had all the information back then because she had wanted his body but not his trust.

Was it too late to come back from this? What did she want from him now?

A divorce. That was what she wanted. She was only with him now under sufferance in order to secure her brother's sponsorship.

He wanted her. That hadn't changed one iota. The desire he felt for her was as strong and powerful as ever—maybe even more so. She'd said she wanted to keep things platonic but he knew she still wanted him as much as he wanted her. He didn't want her to come back at him when the month was up and accuse him of coercing her into having sex with him. He wanted her to come to him because she owned and accepted her need of him. That she was fully engaged in their 'affair' because it was what *she* wanted.

His conscience gave him a prod about the use of the word *affair*. An affair was temporary, but that was all he was prepared to offer now. Letting anyone, particularly Ailsa, have that much power over him was anathema to him. He was back to being an affair man again. Short-term and satisfying, that was how he'd liked his relationships in the past and he would learn to like them that way again. His relationships would run to his timetable and be conducted on his terms.

And his relationship with Ailsa would be no different.

Ailsa tried to settle with a book until Vinn came back from the hospital, but her mind was whirling and her body still restless, aching for the weight of his arms. She was annoyed with herself for not being able to switch off her desire for him. She felt guilty her restlessness came not from her worry over Dom's condition but for the aching need Vinn had awakened in her body. Every time he touched her it ramped up her desire another notch.

It was strange to admit it, but she knew if they hadn't got talking about his father's death so soon after her leaving him, and her confession about the secret she had been keeping all these years, they would have made love again by now. She had been so close to capitulating. She had resigned herself to another quick scratch of the itch. The itch he alone generated in her flesh.

But then he'd told her about his father's accident. They had actually talked. Not just talked but *communicated*. He had allowed her to see the difficult situation he'd been in back then. The situation she had placed him in with her childish storming off. For almost two years she had seethed with anger at the way he had simply let her walk out of his life. Her anger had sustained her; it had motivated her to get her own business up and running. She had directed all those negative emotions into creating beauty and elegance in her clients' homes. Priding herself on how successful she had become in such a short time, not realising her most valuable clients had come her way via Vinn.

And now she had told him what she had told no one about her background. She had shared with him her pain and shame and he hadn't been revolted by her but rather by the situation. By the crime that was committed and the fact no justice was ever served.

You should have told him two years ago.

Ailsa closed her ears to the nudge of her conscience. She hadn't been ready two years ago. And anyway, they hadn't had that sort of relationship. They had communicated with their bodies but not their hearts and minds. She had allowed herself to be rushed into marriage because their lust for each other had been overwhelming. Vinn's passion for her had taken her by surprise, as had hers for him.

It had been like an explosion the first time they'd made love. Nothing in her experience could have prepared her for it. In the past, sex was something a partner did to her and, while she had sometimes enjoyed the physical closeness, until she'd made love with Vinn, full satisfying pleasure had mostly escaped her. But Vinn's expertise in bed had put an end to her orgasm drought. She'd become aware of her body's potential for pleasure and felt proud of the pleasure she brought to him. She liked to think he hadn't felt such intense pleasure with anyone else, but she knew it was fanciful thinking on her part. As soon as they were officially divorced he would be off with another partner.

It still surprised her he hadn't already done so.

Was it more fanciful thinking to hope he cared for her? That he had in fact loved her and loved her still and wanted her back in his life? If so, why was he insisting it be a temporary affair? She'd convinced him to cut it down to one month instead of three. Surely if he wanted her back permanently he would have said so? He had enough bargaining power with Isaac's sponsorship. He knew she would do just about anything for her younger brother.

But what if this was a plan for revenge? What if Vinn wanted her back long enough to make her fall in love with him all over again? What if his plan was to hurt her pride, the way his pride was hurt when she'd walked out of their marriage? He might feel sorry for the circumstances of her background but she knew him well enough to know that wouldn't be enough to distract him from a goal. If he wanted revenge then what better tool than to have her fall for him, *properly* fall for him?

Not just in lust but in life-changing, long-lasting love.

Vinn sat by his grandfather's bedside in ICU for a couple of hours but, apart from a brief flicker of Nonno's eyelids and a weak grasp of his hand when he'd first arrived, the old man had been sleeping ever since. The transplant team were cautiously optimistic about his grandfather's condition but Vinn couldn't quite quell a lingering sense of impending doom. The hospital sounds scraped at his nerves, bringing back memories he thought he had locked away. Even the squeak of a nurse's shoes along the corridor was enough to get his heart racing and his skin to break out in beads of sweat.

It wasn't that he didn't expect to lose his grandfather at some point. It was normal to outlive both your parents and grandparents, but still... Nonno was the only relative—the only person—Vinn trusted.

The only person he loved.

The only person he *allowed* himself to love.

What about Ailsa?

Vinn frowned at the thought of how he was fooling his grandfather about his relationship with Ailsa. Nonno had always liked her. He admired her spirit and feistiness and the way she stood up to Vinn. The only reason Vinn had orchestrated this charade was because of his grandfather's affection for Ailsa.

It had nothing to do with him—with *his* feelings for her, which right at this point in time were a little confusing, to say the least.

For the last twenty-two months he'd been simmering and brooding with anger about the way she'd ended their relationship. He had concentrated on those negative feelings to the point of ignoring the presence of others. Other feelings he had ruthlessly suppressed because allowing himself to love someone exposed him to the potential for hurt.

For loss.

He was fine with the one-month plan. He had cut it down from three because he was not an unreasonable man. He was a business owner himself so he knew the difficulties of running a business at arm's length. One month with Ailsa gave him enough time to get his grandfather out of danger and stable and well enough to cope with the truth about the state of their marriage.

Vinn didn't like thinking beyond the month ahead. But he did know one thing—he would be the one to call time because no way was he going to let Ailsa walk out on him again.

Ailsa was half asleep when she heard Vinn come back from the hospital just after midnight. Keen to find out how his grandfather was doing, she put aside her determination to keep her distance from Vinn and found him standing by the window in his study downstairs. He hadn't even bothered to turn on the lights and was silhouetted by the moonlight.

'Vinn?'

He turned from the window, his features cast in shadow giving him an intimidating air. 'Go back to bed.'

Ailsa stepped further into the room, the floorboards creaking eerily as she moved closer to his tall imposing figure. 'How is your grandfather? Were you able to speak to him?'

'Not really.' He pushed a hand back over his forehead, making his hair even more tousled as if it hadn't been the first time that night he'd done so. 'He was conscious for a bit but heavily dosed up with painkillers so went straight back to sleep.'

She moved closer so she could touch him on the arm. 'Are you okay?'

He gave her a vestige of a smile and a crooked one at that. 'It's tough…seeing him like that. So…so helpless, hovering between life and death.'

'Are the doctors happy with his progress so far?'

Vinn took her hand off his arm and, turning

it over, began absently stroking the middle of her palm with his thumb. 'Yes, so far, but who can predict how these things will go? There are risks with any surgery and this is one hell of an operation, especially for a man that age.'

Ailsa began her own absent stroking of his hand, well, maybe it wasn't so absent for she couldn't resist the feel of his skin under her touch—the warmth of it, the way his fingers were so long and tanned compared to hers. 'Carlotta told me a little bit about your mother. How lovely she was and how much she loved you.'

He frowned. 'When did you see her? I thought she was having the week off.'

'She came earlier today when you were out,' Ailsa said. 'She brought in some shopping but she didn't stay long. I got the feeling she wanted to see if I was really back or not.'

'Did you argue with her?'

She tried not to be annoyed by the way he so readily took his housekeeper's side. 'No, not really.'

One of his eyebrows lifted. 'What's that supposed to mean?'

Ailsa blew out a small breath and pulled her hand out of his hold. 'Look, I understand

your connection with her and I also understand hers to you. She genuinely cares about
you and wants you to be happy. I guess she
realises, and did right from the start, that you
would not be happy with me in the long-term.'

'Why would she think that?'

'Because... I don't love you.' Ailsa's mouth
said the words but her heart wasn't in agreement. Why had it taken her so long to realise
the depth of her feelings for him?

Something flickered across his features.
'Did you tell her that?'

'I didn't have to,' Ailsa said. 'She figured
it out for herself. She thinks I married you to
bolster my self-esteem.'

He took her left hand and ran the pad of
his thumb over the setting of diamonds of her
engagement ring. 'And is that why you married me, *cara*?' His voice was low and deep
and with just the right amount of huskiness
to make her spine loosen.

Ailsa looked into his dark-as-pitch gaze and
wondered that he couldn't see it for himself.
That along with her need to boost her self-esteem there had been another reason she had
married him. A reason she had denied and disguised because if she admitted, even to herself,

that she loved him it would make her decision to remain childless all the more heartbreaking. 'This is why I married you.' She stepped up on tiptoe and pressed her lips to his.

His hands settled on her hips, drawing her closer as he took control of the kiss. His tongue came in search of hers, making her whimper as his body stirred and thickened against hers. His stubble grazed her face as he changed position but she didn't care. She was hungry for his touch. She was aching in every cell of her body for his possession. No one kissed her the way he did. No one made her senses sing the way he did. No one could trigger this torrent of lust the way he did. Her hands went to the buttons of his shirt, tearing at them with careless disregard for their welfare. She wanted him with a fierce need that clawed at her insides. And if the surging potency of him pressing against her was any indication, he wanted her just as badly. Just as ferociously.

Ailsa was only wearing a silky wrap and a slip of a nightgown and soon it was on the floor in a silken puddle at her feet. His ruined shirt joined it and then his trousers and underwear and socks and shoes. Then she was on the floor on her back without any real memory of how she got there as she was so intent on devouring his mouth and clutching at his hard male flesh.

'We should slow down or things will get out of—'

'Don't you dare slow down.' Ailsa dug her hands into the taut muscles of his buttocks and held him to her pulsing need. 'I want you. *Now.*'

He smiled against her mouth and drove into her with a gasp-inducing thrust that made every intimate muscle in her body weep with relief. He set a fast pace but she was with him all the way, panting and clawing and whimpering as the sensations built like a tornado approaching. She could feel the carpet burning the back of her shoulders but she was beyond caring. The need for release was so overwhelming she thought she might die if it didn't come soon.

And then she was there when he added that extra friction with his fingers against her swollen clitoris. She came with a cry that sounded so primal and wild she could hardly believe it came from her throat. Her body bucked and thrashed beneath his with the force of her orgasm, waves and waves rolling through her. His release came on the tail-end of hers, the sheer power of it reverberating through her flesh, his deep agonised groan as primal-sounding as hers.

Ailsa lay panting on the floor under the press of his now relaxed body, her hands moving up and down his back and shoulders in the quiet of the afterglow. The moonlight shone in from the window, casting their entwined bodies in a ghostly light. It could well have been two years ago after one of their passionate lovemaking sessions…but this time somehow it felt different. She couldn't explain it… Perhaps it was because he knew about her background and the sheer relief of not having to hide that from him any more made her feel freer, less weighted. Less abnormal.

Vinn propped himself up on his arms and looked into her eyes. 'I didn't rush you too much?'

Ailsa gave him a lopsided smile and brushed some tousled strands of his hair back off his face. 'I'm fine apart from some mild carpet burn and stubble rash.'

Concern shadowed his gaze and he moved his weight off her and gently turned her so her back was facing him. He brought his mouth down to both of her shoulder blades in turn, pressing soft soothing kisses to the skin. She couldn't remember a time when he had been so tender, as if she were something precious and fragile and he couldn't bear to hurt her even if inadvertently. He turned her back over so she was face up and then he softly ran a fingertip over the circle of skin on her chin. 'I keep forgetting how sensitive you are.'

'My skin might be but I'm certainly not.' It was a lie and she was sure he knew it.

His finger circled her still tingling mouth, his gaze thoughtful as it held hers. 'I'm not so sure you're as tough as you make everyone think.'

Ailsa worried he might see more than she wanted him to see, like how she was falling back in love with him. But maybe a part of her had always been in love with him. Now that part was growing, expanding, swelling inside her until there was no room for the hate she had claimed to feel for him.

She averted her gaze from his and focused her attention instead on the dip at the base of his neck between his clavicles, tracing her finger down from there to his sternum. 'Are we going to lie here on the floor all night or go up to bed?'

Vinn tipped up her chin so her gaze had to meet his. 'Which bed are you thinking of occupying? Mine or the spare bedroom?'

Ailsa gave him a rueful twist of her mouth. 'Do I have a choice?'

'That depends.' He brushed her lips with his, once, twice, three times.

She ran her tongue over her tingling lips and tasted his salt. 'On what?'

He wound a strand of her hair around one of his fingertips, his eyes still holding hers with quiet intensity. 'On whether we're talking about my willpower or yours?'

Ailsa sent her fingertip down his abdomen to the hardened length of him, circling him with her fingers, moving the pad of her thumb over the moist tip where his body was signalling its readiness to mate. 'How's yours doing so far?'

His dark eyes glinted. 'It's toast,' he said and his mouth came down on hers.

CHAPTER EIGHT

THE FOLLOWING EVENING on their way back from visiting his grandfather at the hospital, Vinn suggested a night out. 'Just like old times.'

Ailsa wasn't so sure she wanted to go back to the 'old times'. It had been fun going out for dinner at amazing restaurants were they were waited on like royalty and to nightclubs or exclusive bars, but when had they talked to each other on those occasions? She wanted to know more about his mother's death and how it had impacted on him. And even though it intensified her guilt over leaving him the way she had, she wanted to know more about his father's accident and how he'd juggled everything in the aftermath.

She waited until they were seated in one of the restaurants where they'd dined in the past, with drinks in front of them and their meals ordered, before she brought up the subject. 'Vinn... I've been wondering how you managed everything when your father died. Your work, your grandfather's grief. The other accident victims.'

His expression flickered like he was masking deep physical pain. He seemed to waver for a moment, as if he was torn between wanting to change the subject and offloading some of the burden he'd gone through. 'It was difficult...' He paused for a beat. 'Different from when my mother died. I felt guilty about that, actually. That I wasn't grieving for my father the way I had for my mother. I don't miss him even now and yet not a day goes past without me thinking of her.'

Ailsa reached across the table and laid her hand on the top of his, her voice choking up as if it were her own mother she had lost. 'Oh, Vinn. You must have loved her so much and you were so terribly young.'

He turned over her hand and covered it with his. 'Even though I was young, I remember everything about her. Her smile, her hugs, the way she lit up a room when she walked into it.' His fingers began playing with hers. 'When my father injured those other innocent people

I couldn't get them out of my mind. The kids, I mean, not just the parents, although that was bad enough. I couldn't bear the thought of those little kids growing up without their mother.'

Ailsa realised yet again how stupid and immature she had been to leave the way she had. Why hadn't she been there for him? Helping him, supporting him through such a harrowing time? 'I can't imagine how dreadful it must have been for you and for them. But they survived, yes?'

'Yes.' His hand briefly squeezed hers. 'I sent them presents at Christmas. I wasn't sure if they'd accept them, given it was my father who nearly destroyed their family, but they seem to like me contacting them. I think it helps them put it behind them. Or at least I hope so.'

'I'm sure it helps enormously,' Ailsa said. 'It shows what a generous and caring person you are.'

He gave a stiff on-off smile and withdrew his hand. 'But it still doesn't change the fact my father almost killed them. But he did kill his girlfriend and no amount of Christmas presents or financial compensation will ever make up for that.'

Ailsa's heart squeezed at the way he carried such a burden of guilt and shame about his father even now. 'You weren't driving that car, Vinn. That was your father. You've done everything you can to help those poor people. So many people in your situation wouldn't have done half of what you've done for them.'

Their meals arrived and the conversation switched to less emotionally charged topics. But after their main meal and dessert was cleared, Vinn reached for her hand and began a gentle stroking of her fingers. 'Have you ever tried to talk to your mother about what happened to her? How it affected her and, consequently, her parenting of you?'

Ailsa began to chew at her lower lip. 'She doesn't like talking about it. Michael wanted her to get counselling but she always refused.' She looked at Vinn's tanned fingers entwined with hers. 'I never understood it as a little kid, but whenever I needed a hug from my mother she would pull away from me. It was as if she couldn't bear to touch me. It hurt so much so I taught myself not to need hugs.'

His fingers gave hers a brief squeeze. 'Can you see it wasn't about you? That it was the trauma she associated with you that was the issue? That you're not personally to blame?'

Ailsa met his gaze. 'I do on an intellectual level but on an emotional level I still feel like that little kid needing a hug from her mum and being pushed away.'

Vinn cradled her hand so tenderly she felt like he was reaching back in time to her as that needy little child, offering her comfort and security. 'Do you think if you talked to your mother about your own issues with having a family it might help you and even her?'

Ailsa gave a non-committal shrug without speaking. What was the point of talking to her mother? It wouldn't change the fact she was the offspring of a criminal. No one could change that. She had to learn to live with it.

Vinn's fingers gently tapped her on the back of the hand as if to bring her out of her private reverie. 'Time to go home, or do you want coffee?'

Ailsa didn't want the evening to end. She had never felt so close to someone as she did right then. Not just a physical closeness, but an emotional closeness where walls had been lowered and screens and masks laid aside. Would this newfound intimacy between them last? What would happen when their month was up? What then? She gave him a tentative smile. 'No coffee for me.'

What I want is you.

Later, when they got home, Vinn reached for her without saying a word. His mouth came down on hers and his arms gathered her close. Their lovemaking was slow but intense, as if he was discovering her body's secrets all over again. There was an element of poignancy to his caresses and touches. They made her feel as if she was so much more than a woman he had wanted to marry because she ticked all the boxes. He made her feel as if she was the only woman he wanted to make love to. He might not love her the way she had grown to love him, but it was enough for her now to be held close enough for their hearts to beat against each other. Close enough for her to feel as if the last two painful years hadn't happened.

Close enough for her to feel as if she had finally come home.

Two weeks later, when Ailsa woke, she was starting to wonder how she would ever return to London and her former life of work, work and more work. Her days had formed a pattern of her sleeping in while Vinn rose early to see to his business commitments, then he would come back for her mid-morning so they could visit his grandfather together.

Dom was now fully awake and out of ICU and in a private room and, while he was still frail, at least he no longer had a jaundiced look about him. She was glad for him and for Vinn, for she could see the bond between them was strong and she couldn't help envying it. She had never felt close to her mother or stepfather and since both sets of grandparents had always lived abroad and two were now deceased, they hadn't been as involved with her and Isaac as much as other grandparents might have been. She was close to Isaac in that she loved him and would do anything for him but he didn't know her as well as he might think. And she didn't want him to. She couldn't bear him finding out she was only his half-sister.

Another thing that had happened over the last few days was an unspoken truce between her and Carlotta. The elderly housekeeper came in the morning soon after Vinn left for his office and only stayed long enough to tidy whatever needed tidying. She didn't cook the evening meal as she used to before as Ailsa had insisted she and Vinn would eat out most evenings and any evening they didn't she would cook. If Carlotta was annoyed to find her services were not required in the same capacity as before, she certainly didn't show it. If anything, Ailsa thought Carlotta was privately pleased she had stepped up to the wifely role she had been resisting two years ago with such vehemence.

She lay back against the pillows on Vinn's bed and sighed. It was increasingly hard to find the strong-willed career girl who had fallen in lust with Vinn. In her place was a mellow version, a woman who was content to listen instead of spout an opinion, a woman who was dangerously close to wanting much more than she could ever have. She tried to console herself that once this month was up she would have ten million reasons to be content and happy with her lot in life. She was so much better off than most people. She had no right to be hankering after the fairy tale when she was not the daughter of royalty but the daughter of darkness.

Ailsa threw the covers off the bed and got to her feet but the room started to spin and she had to sit down again before she fell down. Her stomach had a queasy feeling, a low-grade nausea that was annoying rather than debilitating. She waited for a moment or two before rising tentatively to her feet. *So far so good.* The room had stopped spinning but her stomach was still unsettled. She showered and dressed, deciding she'd better pull herself together before Vinn got back from the office, not wanting to add to his worries about his grandfather.

Carlotta was in the kitchen when Ailsa came downstairs and narrowed her bird-like gaze when Ailsa came in. 'Are you unwell? You look pale.'

Ailsa put a hand on her stomach. 'It must be something I ate last night when we went out for dinner. Too much rich food.'

Carlotta's expression was difficult to read, which was unusual because usually she had no qualms about showing what she felt, be it disapproval, censure or a grudging acceptance. 'Sit down, Signora Gagliardi,' she said, pulling out a chair. 'I will make you a cup of tea and some dry toast.'

Ailsa sat down but her mind kept tiptoeing around the reason why Carlotta would offer to make her tea and dry toast. There was no way she could be pregnant. She still had a contraceptive implant in her arm. Yes, it was a little overdue for a change but she hadn't had a normal period since she'd had it implanted so it must still be working. A flutter of panic beat inside her belly and she put a hand over her abdomen in an effort to quell it. It had to be still working.

It *had* to.

Carlotta turned from switching on the kettle and Ailsa wasn't quite quick enough to remove her hand in time to escape the quick flick of the housekeeper's gaze. 'Will you tell him?'

Ailsa swallowed. 'Tell him what?'

'That you're having his *bambino*.'

She choked out a laugh. 'I'm not having his—'

'So it's not his child?'

Ailsa was struck dumb by the housekeeper's insinuation. She suddenly felt close to tears. This couldn't be happening. Not now. Not ever. She couldn't have Vinn's baby. She couldn't allow herself to dream of holding his child in her arms, of being with him permanently. He didn't want her for ever anyway. This was just for now, until his grandfather was well enough to handle the truth.

This was not part of the plan.

Carlotta came over with a steaming cup of tea and set in on the table in front of Ailsa. 'Drink it. The toast will be ready in a minute. Nibble on it slowly until your stomach settles.'

Ailsa wasn't sure if it was the nurturing the housekeeper was dishing out or the stress she was feeling about the possibility of being pregnant that made her emotions suddenly spill over. One sob rose in her throat and another closely followed it, then another and another until she sat with her head in her hands and with her shoulders shaking. 'This can't be happening… I can't do this… I can't have a baby. I just can't.'

Carlotta stroked the top of Ailsa's head with a touch so gentle it made her cry all the more. 'You are lucky to be with child. I would have given anything to have a *bambino* of my own but it wasn't to be. My husband left me because of it.'

Ailsa dragged her face out of her hands to look at the housekeeper's wistful expression.

'I'm sorry you weren't able to have children. I really am. But I've never wanted to have them. My career is too important to me.'

Carlotta brushed the hair back off Ailsa's face like she was a child, her gaze soft and full of wisdom. 'Have you really always not wanted to have children?'

Ailsa gave a shaky sigh and dropped her head back into her hands. 'Not always…but it's complicated and I don't want to talk about it.'

'He'll make a good father,' Carlotta said, still stroking the back of Ailsa's head. 'He won't be reckless and irresponsible like his father. He'll support you and the child—'

'But will he love me?' Ailsa looked up at her again.

Carlotta's expression became sombre. 'He might not say it the way other men would but he cares about you. Why else would he have asked you to come back to him?'

Ailsa got to her feet, holding onto the edge of the table in case she felt another wave of faintness. 'Please, I beg you. Don't tell him about this. I need to make sure first.'

'You're not going to get rid of—?'

'No,' Ailsa said, realising with a jolt it was

true. 'No, I can't do that. It might be right for some people and I would never judge them for it, but it's not right for me.'

'But he has the right to know as soon as—'

'I'll cross that bridge if and when I come to it,' Ailsa said. 'This could be a false alarm. I don't want to get his hopes up. It would cause more hurt in the long run.'

Carlotta didn't look too convinced but she agreed to keep silent on the subject. 'Is there anything I can do for you, Signora Gagliardi?'

Ailsa attempted a smile but couldn't quite pull it off. 'Yes, call me Ailsa.'

Carlotta smiled back. 'Ailsa.'

Ailsa went back upstairs but, instead of going back to the master bedroom, she went to the one room she hadn't visited since she'd been back. The door was closed and she hadn't once been tempted to open it but now she held her breath and turned the doorknob and stepped inside. It was exactly the same as the last time she'd walked out of it with her ears stubbornly plugged against Vinn's suggestion they talk about having a family. It was the only room in the villa that was unfinished... incomplete, like an interrupted conversation. She looked at the room with new eyes, not seeing its potential as a reading room but as Vinn had seen it—as a nursery. A nursery for the child she might be carrying.

His child.

She looked at the empty space and in her mind's eye saw a white cradle with a pastel-coloured animal mobile dangling overhead. She saw soft toys—teddy bears and kittens and puppies and cute long-eared rabbits sitting on the shelf above the fireplace, next to a row of picture books and childhood classics. She saw neatly folded baby clothes—most of them handmade—in the chest of drawers.

And in the window…a rocking chair perfect for feeding or settling a baby…

Ailsa drew in a breath that pulled on something deep in her chest and turned and left the room, quietly closing the door behind her.

Vinn was late getting back to the villa to collect Ailsa to visit his grandfather. Work had been piling up while he'd been spending so much time with her and there were a few pressing meetings and some urgent paperwork he'd needed to see to. He was used to spending most of his time at work. Even during their marriage he had prioritised work over his time at home. He was always conscious of how close to losing everything he had been when his father had been convicted of fraud. It was a driving force inside him he had little or no control over. Working hard was in his blood as it was in his grandfather's and his great-grandfather's before him.

When he finally got back to the villa it was closer to lunch than he'd realised. He found Ailsa sitting outside in the garden with a magazine lying across her lap but she was staring into space rather than reading it. She gave a little start of surprise when she heard his footsteps on the flagstones and sprang out of the garden seat but then seemed to stumble and almost fell.

He rushed to stabilise her with a hand on her arm. '*Cara*, what's wrong?'

She squinted against the strong sunlight and leaned on him for support. 'It's hotter out here than I realised...'

It didn't feel hot to Vinn but then he was used to Milan in spring, which on balance was generally much warmer than what she'd be used to in London. 'Sit down for a bit here in the shade.' He guided her back to the garden seat and crouched down in front of her with his hands resting on her knees. 'Feeling better now?'

She gave him a funny little smile and her gaze kept skipping away from his. 'Yep, much better now.'

She certainly didn't look it. She had a waxen look to her features and there were tiny beads of perspiration around her temples. Vinn placed a hand on her forehead to check if she had a temperature but, while she was clammy to touch, she wasn't burning with a fever that he could tell. 'Maybe you shouldn't come with me to visit Nonno today. You must have a virus or something.'

'Okay…'

He stood and held out his hand to help her to her feet. 'Come on, *tesoro*. Let's get you inside and resting. I'll call the doctor to come round and—'

'No!' There was a shrill note of panic in her tone. 'I… I don't need to see a doctor. It's just a bug or…or something…' She bit down on her lip and for a moment he thought she was going to cry.

He put his hands on the tops of her shoulders. 'Are you sure you're okay, *cara*?'

'I just need to lie down for a while…'

Vinn helped her upstairs and got her settled in bed with a long cool drink beside her. 'I won't be long. I'll just check in on Nonno and come back to see how you're feeling.'

'Okay...'

Ailsa waited until she heard the sound of Vinn's car leaving the driveway before she threw off the light bedcovers he had drawn over her moments ago. Sick or not, she had to get her hands on a pregnancy test. Two or more tests. Possibly more. She felt a little guilty ducking out of the villa while he thought she was safely tucked up in bed but what else could she do?

She had to know, one way or the other.

The streets were crowded enough for her to blend in without being recognised...or so she hoped. She'd tied her hair back and pulled on a baseball cap and dressed in tracksuit pants and a T-shirt, making her look as if she was just out for a walk or a trip to the gym. She went into the first pharmacy she came to and bought two test kits, figuring if she bought too many from the one place it might draw too much attention to herself. She was about to walk into another pharmacy when she bumped into a man who was coming out. She mumbled an apology and went to sidestep him but he called her by name.

'Ailsa? I thought it was you hiding under that disguise.'

Ailsa looked up to see one of Vinn's acquaintances, Nico Di Sante, the owner of the hotel she had checked into on her first night in Milan two weeks ago. What quirk of fate had led her to that hotel and now to the very same pharmacy he was using? 'Oh…hi…'

His gaze narrowed. 'Are you okay?'

Ailsa tried to relax her tight features. 'Sure. I'm just trying to get some errands done without being recognised. You know what the paps are like.'

'Sure do.'

She shifted her weight from foot to foot, not wanting to extend their conversation past the greeting stage, but neither did she want to appear rude or draw unnecessary attention to herself. 'Well…it was nice seeing you again.'

'You too, Ailsa,' Nico said. 'Hey, I'm really glad you guys are back together. Vinn's really missed you.' He gave a short laugh. 'Not that he would ever admit it to anyone. He's too proud for that. Stubborn too.'

Ailsa managed a small smile. 'I missed him too.'

'Tell him to bring you in for cocktails in my new bar.' Nico smiled. 'On the house, of course.'

Ailsa stretched her mouth into an answering smile. 'Will do.'

But she had a horrible feeling it might be several months before she would be drinking alcohol again. Was this how her mother had felt, finding out she was pregnant? Feeling dread and shock and anguish instead of joy and excitement? She couldn't help feeling a wave of sadness for her mother. For how isolated and desperate she must have felt, unable to tell anyone what had happened to her and then the double blow of finding out she was pregnant. Her mother had said it had been too late to have a termination but why hadn't she put her up for adoption instead?

Maybe Vinn was right—she should try and talk to her mother. Even if she shut down the conversation, at least Ailsa would have tried instead of letting things go on the way they were for God knew how many more years.

She took out her phone on the walk back to Vinn's villa. She had never felt the need to talk to her mother as she did then and a wave of relief flooded her when she finally picked up on the seventh ring. 'Mum?'

'Ailsa...' Her mother sounded a little distracted and Ailsa wondered if she had someone with her. A new man in her life perhaps?

'Is this a bad time to call?'

'No, of course not.'

'Mum...can I ask you something?'

'What's wrong? You sound upset. Is everything working out between you and—?'

Ailsa took a steadying breath. 'Why didn't you have me adopted? Did you ever think of—?'

'I did think of it...in the early days, but as the pregnancy went on I felt I couldn't do it.'

'So you...you *wanted* me?'

'I would be lying if I said I was completely happy about being pregnant,' her mother said. 'I wasn't the earth mother type. I wanted children but I probably wouldn't have been miserable without them either. But about six months into the pregnancy I knew I would never be able to let you go to someone else. But why are you asking me this now?'

'Mum, I think I'm pregnant,' Ailsa said. 'I don't know what to do.'

'Have you done a test?'

'Not yet. I just bought one. I just wanted to talk to someone…you, actually.'

'Oh, Ailsa…' Her mother gave a sigh. 'I'm probably not the best person to talk to. I felt so ambivalent about being pregnant with you and I know it's probably affected our relationship but—'

'I know and that's completely understandable,' Ailsa said. 'It must have been awful, so terrifying to know you had to carry a child you didn't want to term.'

'It wasn't just because of the…because of what happened,' her mother said. 'I was the same when I fell pregnant with Isaac. I'm not the nurturing type. I feel ashamed of it but I can't change it. It's hardwired into my personality. But it doesn't mean I don't love you and Isaac. I don't regret going ahead with the pregnancy. It was hard and I was in denial for a long time about how it affected me, but I'm glad I had you. I guess I'm not that good at showing it. But maybe you can help me work on that… I mean, if you'd like to?'

'I would love to,' Ailsa said, suddenly overcome with emotion. 'I'll do the test and let you know the results, okay?'

She ended the call with a bubble of hope expanding in her chest. Hope for a better relationship with her mother, hope for a future with Vinn.

Hope for a child.

Vinn's trip to the hospital to visit his grandfather was cut short because Nonno's specialists were doing a ward round. His grandfather had developed a slight temperature overnight and since Ailsa had some sort of virus, in spite of the thoroughness of the hygiene procedure on entering the ward, he thought it would be best to come back the following day when his grandfather was feeling better. His grandfather seemed more concerned about Ailsa than his own health when Vinn told him.

'Send her my love and tell her I hope she feels better soon,' Nonno said.

'Will do. Take care of yourself. I'll be in tomorrow and Ailsa will too if she's feeling well enough.'

Vinn decided to swing by a local florist on his way home and pick up some flowers for Ailsa. She'd looked so peaky and unwell and he thought a bunch of spring flowers would lift her spirits.

Two weeks had passed and he was becoming more and more conscious of the clock ticking on their relationship. It was way too early to know if his grandfather was out of danger—there were always things that could go wrong and he was still being closely monitored. Vinn wished now he'd insisted on the three months as he'd first proposed. That would have given him ample time to get his grandfather out of hospital and set up in the independent living apartment he'd bought for him so there would be twenty-four-hour medical care on hand.

Could he ask Ailsa to reconsider? They could come to some arrangement if she needed to go back to London for work. He could even go with her as he'd long thought about setting up a UK branch of his furniture business.

His mind started to run with the possibility of postponing the divorce, even taking it off the table altogether. They were a functional couple now. They communicated better than they ever had before and their sex life was as good, if not better, than when they were first married. And now that Ailsa had told him about her background, he realised how wrong it would have been to bring children into their marriage back then. But could he settle for a life without children? Could he take the risk that she might never change her mind?

His grandfather was in the winter of his life and his greatest wish was for a great-grand-child to hold before he died. But it was Vinn's wish too. He wanted to hold his own child in his arms, to share the bond of a child with Ailsa because he couldn't imagine wanting a child with anyone else.

But she doesn't love you.

Vinn shoved the thought aside. What did romantic love have to do with it? That sort of love was fleeting anyway. It often didn't last beyond the honeymoon phase of a relation-ship. Caring for someone, providing for them, sharing your life with them and creating and raising a family with them required commit-ment and steadfastness and maturity.

Two years ago, he hadn't understood Ail-sa's reluctance to commit to having a family. But he did now and he couldn't see any reason why they couldn't work through it and, even if they didn't end up having kids, at least they would have made that decision together. Their relationship had undergone a change, a remod-elling that made him look forward to coming home to her. He might not love her in the Hollywood movie sense but he damn well cared about her and wanted her in his life.

Not just for a month. Not just for three months.

For ever.

CHAPTER NINE

AILSA WAS IN one of the guest bathrooms upstairs when she heard Vinn's footsteps on the stairs. Her heart began to race. She hadn't had time to do the test; she had barely had time to read the instructions. What was he doing home so soon? Normally he stayed a couple of hours at the hospital with his grandfather. She quickly bundled the test back into the paper bag and shoved it into the cupboard under the marble basin.

'Ailsa?' Vinn's knuckles rapped on the bathroom door. 'Are you okay?'

She took a calming breath. 'Yes…j-just finishing up in here.' She flushed the toilet and then turned on the taps in the guise of washing her hands. Her hand crept to her abdomen… She had always been so adamant about not wanting children but she had never been pregnant before, or even suspected she was pregnant.

What if Vinn's DNA was this very minute getting it on with hers? What if a tiny being was being fashioned inside her womb, a tiny embryo that would one day lift up its little chubby arms and call her Mummy?

Ailsa bit her lip so hard she thought she'd break the skin. It wasn't supposed to happen like this. She'd been fine with her decision not to have kids when she wasn't pregnant. Falling pregnant changed everything.

It changed *her*.

'Ailsa. Open the door.'

Her heart leapt to her throat and pushed out the sob she'd been holding there. 'Go away. I'll be out in a minute.'

'No. I will not go away.' Vinn's voice had a steely edge to it that made her heart thump all the harder.

Ailsa blew out a breath, put on her game face and opened the door. 'What does a girl have to do around here to get a little privacy?'

His concerned gaze ran over her. 'Why have you locked yourself in here? Have you been sick?'

Ailsa found it hard to hold his gaze. How could she tell him before she knew for sure? Or should she tell him? It was a set of scales tipping back and forth inside her head—*Tell him. Don't tell him. Tell him. Don't tell him.* She let go of a breath she hadn't realised she'd been holding. 'I... I went to the pharmacy.'

'I have painkillers here if only you'd asked me to—'

'Not for painkillers.' She took another breath and let it out in a rush. 'For a pregnancy test.'

Shock rippled over his features, but then his eyes lit up and a broad smile broke over his face. 'You're pregnant? Really? But, *tesoro*, that's wonderful. I was on my way home to ask you to call off the divorce so we can start again.'

He wanted to start again? Oh, the irony of his timing. Had he made that decision before or just now when he thought there was a chance she could be pregnant? How could she trust his offer was centred on his feelings for her, not his family-making plans? How could she accept knowing the one thing he wanted was a child, not the mother who came with it—her?

'I haven't done the test yet,' Ailsa said. 'I was about to when you started hammering on the door.'

He took her by the upper arms in a gentle hold, his face still wreathed in a smile. 'Sorry about that, *cara*. I was worried about you. Let's do the test now, shall we? It'll be fun doing it together—finding out at the same moment.'

Ailsa chewed at her lip. 'Don't get too excited, Vinn.'

His fingers tightened on her arms. 'You're not thinking about terminating?'

She pulled out of his hold and rubbed at her arms as if his touch had hurt her. 'Don't be ridiculous. Of course I'm not going to terminate.'

He reached for her again and his hands began a slow stroke of her arms. 'Let's do the test so we know one way or the other.'

Ailsa sighed and, pulling away, walked back to the bathroom where she'd stashed the test kits. He waited outside while she collected the sample of urine and then she opened the door again so he could join her as the test was processed.

'Is that two lines?' Vinn said, standing so close to her she could feel him all but shaking with excitement.

'No, it's too early.' Ailsa could feel her stomach doing cartwheels, her emotions in such turmoil she could barely breathe. It was as if she were holding her destiny in her hands. Two lines would mean she was to become a mother. Two lines that would change her life for ever.

There weren't two lines.

The wand stayed negative.

Ailsa could feel Vinn's disappointment by the way his breath left his body. She could feel her own disappointment coursing through her, making it hard for her to process her emotions. She should be feeling relieved, not disappointed. This was good news…wasn't it?

No. Because the one thing she wanted was a baby. But not with a man who didn't love her, who only wanted her now because she was the one who got away.

She didn't just want a baby. She wanted Vinn to love her the way she loved him. The way she had always loved him. How could she settle for a rerun of their marriage when nothing had changed? Sure, he knew about her past and she knew a bit more about his, but it hadn't made him fall in love with her. He hadn't said anything about loving her.

'Don't worry, *cara*,' Vinn said, winding an arm around her waist. 'We'll keep trying for a baby. It'll happen sooner or later.'

Ailsa moved out of his hold. 'Vinn, stop. Stop planning my future for me without asking me what *I* want.'

His expression flickered and then reset itself to frowning. 'What are you saying? You wanted that baby. I know you did. I could see it in your eyes, damn it, I could feel it in your body. You're as disappointed as me. I know you are.'

She saw no reason to deny it, not even to herself. The time for denial was over. She had to be clear about what she wanted and not settle for anything less. 'You're right. I do want a baby. But I want to have a baby with a man who loves me more than anything else. You're not that man. You've told me yourself you can never be that man.'

'But we'll be great parents, *cara*,' Vinn said. 'We're great together. So what if neither of us is in love with each other? We want each other, we respect each other. Surely that is something to build on?'

Ailsa let out a frustrated sigh. 'I can't be with a man who refuses to love me. Who fights against it as if it's some sort of deadly virus. I want to be loved for me, Vinn. For *me* with all my faults and foibles.'

'I care about you, Ailsa. You surely don't doubt that?'

'You can't say the words, can you? What is so terrifying about admitting you feel more for me than just caring about my welfare?'

'But I do care about you. I always have—'

She let out a laugh that was borderline hysterical. 'You "care" about me.' She put her fingers up in air quotes. 'What does "care" really mean? I'll tell you what it means. It means you don't love me. It means you won't love me. You're not capable or not willing to love me.'

'But you don't love me either so what's the problem?'

Ailsa shook her head at him, exasperated by his inability to see what was staring him in the face. But she wasn't going to say it. She wasn't going to tell him she loved him only for him to throw that love back in her face. To have him cheapen her love by offering a relationship that was loveless. 'I'm going back to London, Vinn. Today. I'm sorry if it upsets your grandfather but I'm sure he'll understand I can't do this. I can't be in a marriage like this. I deserve more and so do you.'

Vinn's expression went through various

makeovers. First it looked blank, then angry, then shocked and then back to angry again. 'So. You're leaving.' His tone was clipped as if he was making an enormous effort to control himself. 'You do happen to realise what will happen to your brother's sponsorship if you walk out that door?'

'Yes, but I'm hoping you won't punish Isaac because you and I can't be together,' Ailsa said. 'And as to the money you gave me...of course I'll give it back.'

'Keep it.' His lips were so tight it was as if he was spitting out lemon pips instead of words. 'You've earned it.'

'There's no need to be insulting,' Ailsa said, stung by his cruel words. 'But this is exactly why I'm calling it off now before we end up doing even worse to each other. I don't want our divorce to be long and drawn-out and uncivilised. We can be better than that.'

His look was so cutting Ailsa was surprised she didn't end up in little slices on the floor. 'Civilised you say? Then you married the wrong man.'

And, without another word, he turned and left her with just her regrets and heartbreak for company.

* * *

Vinn was so furious he wanted to punch a hole in the nearest wall. She was leaving. Again. She had called time on their relationship in the same half hour when he'd seen a glimpse of the future they could have had together.

A future with children.

A family.

The family he wanted more than he wanted success.

But no. She was leaving because she had never intended to come back. He had *made* her come back. Lured her and blackmailed her, hoping it would change her mind, hoping it would make her see how good they were together.

So she wanted to be civilised about their divorce, did she? He wasn't feeling too civilised right now. He felt every emotion he had locked down deep inside was about to explode out of him. Was it his fault he couldn't say the words she wanted to hear? Was it his fault he had taught himself not to feel love in case it was taken away? How could he switch the ability to love back on? The loss of his mother so young had permanently changed him. It had flicked a switch inside him and he could no longer find the control board to switch it back on again. Loving and losing were so inextricably linked inside his head that he couldn't untangle them, no matter how hard he tried.

He had been so looking forward to seeing his grandfather with the news of Ailsa's pregnancy. He had pictured it in his mind, imagining how delighted Nonno would be to hear the news of the baby. But there wasn't going to be a baby. There wasn't even going to be a marriage any more.

He had failed.

He had failed to win her back and he had failed his grandfather.

He would have to give Ailsa the divorce. He had no choice, the law saw to that. The only consolation was she would have to wait another two years.

He hoped they would be as miserable for her as the last two had been for him.

Ailsa got off the plane in London with a raging temperature and a splitting headache. The bug that had been masquerading as a baby hit her during the flight and she'd curled up in her seat under a blanket and wondered if she had ever felt this miserable.

No. Never. Not even when she'd left Vinn the first time. This was much harder, much more painful because, along with losing Vinn, she'd lost the future she'd longed for. Why couldn't he love her? Was she so awful, so *abnormal* that he couldn't bring himself to love her?

Even as she'd boarded the plane in Milan she'd hoped he would come after her and tell her he'd made a mistake. But he hadn't. She'd stared at the entrance of the boarding gate as she had stared at the wand of that test kit. Wanting something to happen didn't make it happen. It either happened or it didn't.

Vinn didn't love her and she had best get over her disappointment. She'd done it before and she would do it again.

Even if it damn well killed her.

CHAPTER TEN

VINN WAS DREADING telling his grandfather that Ailsa had left him. He even considered not telling him, but that would be doing what his father had done, pretending everything was fine when it wasn't. Pathetic. But in a strange way now he could understand why his father had kept the news of his mother's condition under wraps. It was too painful to face. His father had tried to spare him from pain in the only way he knew how. By pretending. By lying. By hiding the truth until it could be hidden no longer.

But Vinn had to face Ailsa's leaving him just as he'd had to face his mother's death. It was just as permanent for there was nothing he could do to bring her back. Ailsa didn't love him. And all this time he had fooled himself she was the one with more invested in their relationship.

When Vinn went to the hospital the day after Ailsa had left for London, his grandfather still had a temperature and a change of antibiotic had been arranged. He couldn't help feeling concerned at the frailty of his grandfather's appearance. Would the news he was about to break make things worse? How would he be able to live with himself if he sent Nonno over the edge? But how could he live with himself if he kept up the charade?

'Ailsa not coming in today?' Nonno said, glancing past Vinn's shoulders. 'Is she still feeling a little under the weather?'

Vinn pulled the visitor's chair closer to the bed and sat down and slowly released a breath. 'I don't know how to tell you this, Nonno, but she's gone back to London.'

'For work?'

How easy would it be to lie? All he had to say was yes and give his grandfather another day or two of peace before the ugly truth had to be faced. 'Not just for work,' Vinn said. 'The thing is…we weren't really back together.'

His grandfather put his gnarled hand on Vinn's forearm. 'You think I didn't know that?'

Vinn stared at his grandfather. 'You... *knew*?'

Nonno gave a single nod. 'I appreciate what you tried to do. I know you had my best interests at heart. But you have to want her back for you, not me. Because you can't live without her. Because no one else will fill the space she left.'

Vinn's throat was suddenly so constricted it felt as if he'd swallowed one of the pillows off his grandfather's bed. Two pillows. Plus the mattress. Ailsa had left a space so big and achingly empty his chest felt like it was being carved out with a rusty spoon. The inextricable knot was finally loosened inside him. He hadn't been able to say the words but the feelings were there and could no longer be denied or ignored or masqueraded as anything else. His biggest fear hadn't been falling in love. His biggest fear was losing the only person he had loved with all his heart and soul and body. He had to have the courage to own those feelings. To embrace them and express them. 'I love her, Nonno. But I think I've ruined everything. Again.'

'Have you told her you love her?'

Vinn couldn't meet his grandfather's gaze

and looked down at the wedding ring on his left hand instead. Why hadn't he taken it off by now? *Because you love her and can't bear the thought of never seeing her again.* He loved her. He loved her so damn much he hadn't been able to move on with his life. He hadn't taken off his wedding ring because taking it off would mean finally letting go of the hope. The hope that their marriage still had a chance. That was why he'd sent those Italian clients to her studio. He'd been unwilling to finally sever the connection. He'd clung to whatever thread he could to keep her in his life.

He brought his gaze back to his grandfather's. 'What if I've poisoned that love? What if it's too late?'

'You won't find out by sitting here talking to me,' Nonno said. 'The person you need to talk to is Ailsa.'

Vinn sprang to his feet. 'You're right. But I hate leaving you while you're still in ICU. That infection is worrying your specialists. What if you—?' He couldn't finish the sentence for the lump of emotion in his throat.

Nonno waved his hand towards the door. 'Go. I'll be all right. I'm not ready to leave this world yet.' His eyes twinkled. 'I have one more thing to tick off on my bucket list.'

Ailsa got over her virus but her spirits were still so low she could barely drag herself through the day. Forty-eight hours had passed since she'd left Italy and she hadn't heard anything from Vinn. Not that she'd expected him to contact her. Their relationship was over and the sooner she moved on with her life the better. But, even so, every time the studio door opened, her heart would give an extra beat in the hope Vinn might walk through the door.

She'd sent a text to her mother to let her know there wasn't going to be a baby, and told both her mother and stepfather she had left Vinn because she didn't want them reading about it first in the press. Her mother had replied, saying she would come and see her as soon as she could.

It was lunchtime when the bell at the top of the door tinkled again and Ailsa looked up to see her mother and stepfather come in. Normally when her mother said she would drop by it could mean days and days before it actually happened. Was this a sign things were improving in her relationship with her mother? 'Mum? Dad? Why are you both here?'

Her mother spoke first. 'We were worried about you. And sad about your news about Vinn and you calling it quits. Are you okay? Is there anything we can do?'

Ailsa shook her head and sighed. 'No, there's nothing anyone can do.'

Her mother looked anxious and kept darting glances at Ailsa's stepfather. 'We feel so bad about everything. Me particularly. I know I haven't been the best mother to you. I tried but I was so messed-up after... Well, I should have got some help instead of bottling it up. But that's going to change now so—'

'Mum, it's fine, really. You don't have to apologise.'

'But I want to be closer to you,' her mother said. 'Since your father and I divorced... Sorry, I can't help calling Michael your father even though—'

'It's fine, Mum. Michael *is* my father.' Ailsa turned to face him. 'You're the only father I've ever known and ever wanted.'

Michael blinked back tears and reached for Ailsa's mother's hand. 'Thank you, sweetheart. What your mother is trying to say is

we're working at some stuff. We're both having counselling.'

Ailsa looked at her parents' joined hands
and the light shining in her mother's usually
haunted and shadowed eyes. 'What's going on?'

Her mother gave a sheepish smile. 'I feel
bad saying this when you're going through a
relationship breakup, but your dad and I have
realised we're not happy without each other.'

'But you weren't happy together.'

'That was because we weren't being honest
with each other,' Michael said. 'We're learning how to do that now. I don't want to lose
your mother. I don't want to lose the family
we made together.'

Ailsa couldn't believe her ears. 'So you're
getting remarried?'

'Maybe,' her mother said. 'We're not making any promises. But for now we're enjoying
putting the past aside and moving forward.'

Ailsa hugged both her parents in turn. 'I'm
happy for you.'

She just wished she could put the past aside
and move forward too.

Ailsa was about to close the studio for the day
when she saw Vinn walking towards the front

door. Her breath stalled in her throat and her
hand on the key in the door fell away and went
to her chest, where her heart was threatening
to leap out of her chest. He'd left his grandfather back in Milan to come and see her? What
did it mean? 'Vinn?'

'Can we talk?' Vinn said.

Ailsa stepped back to let him enter and
closed the door behind him. 'Why are you
here? Is your grandfather okay? Oh, God…
don't tell me something's happened.'

He smiled and reached for her hands, holding them within the cradle of his. 'Something
has happened, *cara*. I've finally come to my
senses and realised I love you. Can you forgive me for not telling you sooner?'

Ailsa did a rapid blink. 'You love me?'

He gave her hands a gentle squeeze, his
dark eyes shining. 'So so much. I can't believe it's taken me this long to admit it. I was
too frightened, too cowardly to admit I needed
you, that I loved you so much I couldn't bear
to take off my wedding ring because it was
all I had left of you. That's why I fired Rosa.
She told me I was a fool to let the wife I was
madly in love with go without a fight. I fired
her rather than face up to the truth. And I let

you go—twice. Please say you'll forgive me and come back to me.'

Ailsa was crying and laughing at the same time and threw herself against him, winding her arms around his neck. 'I love you too.'

'You do? You really do? Even after all the stupid mistakes I've made?'

She smiled. 'Of course I do. You don't have to say the words to show it, you know.'

He grinned back. 'True, but given how stubborn and blockheaded I am, I think it'd be wise if you did tell me now and again. At least once or twice a day.'

'I love you.' She pressed a kiss to his mouth. 'I love, love, love you.'

'That's a start.' He pressed a kiss to her lips. 'Stay married to me, *cara?* Please? We don't have to live all the time in Milan. I've been thinking about launching a showroom over here. Maybe you could send some clients my way.'

Ailsa grimaced in shame. 'I feel so bad I deliberately directed clients away from your beautiful designs out of spite. And all the while you were sending me clients. You're a much better person than I am.'

He stroked her face with a tender hand.

'You are a wonderful person, *cara*. Don't ever think you're not.'

Ailsa smiled again. 'I've come to some re-alisations of my own in the last little while. I am much more than my DNA. I might not know who my father is but I know who *I* am and that's all that matters.'

Vinn hugged her close. 'And I love who you are and can't wait to spend the rest of my life proving it to you.'

'I thought you only wanted me because you thought I was pregnant. I wouldn't have left the way I did if I'd known you loved me.'

He gave her a rueful smile. 'I'd actually bought you flowers on my way home that day. I planned to ask you to stay with me. I guess it was a roundabout way of expressing the feel-ings I hadn't yet admitted to myself.'

Ailsa stroked his jaw. 'We've been such fools wasting so much time. We've been mak-ing war instead of making love.'

His dark eyes shone with deep emotion. 'I want you in my life no matter what. Having children is not as important to me as you are. I love you and you'll be more than enough for me.'

Ailsa looked at him through a blurry sheen

of tears. 'Oh, Vinn, I do want a baby. I didn't realise how much until I stood with you in that bathroom with that test wand in my hand.'

'You do? Really?' His hands gripped her so tightly it was almost painful. 'But I don't want you just saying that to appease me.'

'I want to make a family with you, darling,' Ailsa said and gave him a twinkling smile. 'How soon can we get started?'

He gave her an answering smile and brought his mouth down to hers. 'Now.'

EPILOGUE

Three months later...

IT WAS THE most unusual way to find out if a pregnancy test was positive or not but Ailsa didn't care. Unusual because instead of just her and Vinn peering at the test wand in the bathroom with expectant breaths held, Vinn's grandfather and Carlotta and Rosa were waiting in the sitting room downstairs for the results. Rosa had come back to work for Vinn and was such an enormous asset to the company that Vinn had been able to step back a little and spend more time with Ailsa and his grandfather.

Ailsa started to well up when she saw the positive lines appear and Vinn's arm around her waist tightened. 'That looks like a positive to me,' he said, grinning at her. 'What do you think?'

She turned in his embrace and linked her arms around his neck, smiling up at him with such joy filling her heart she thought it would burst. 'I think you are going to be the best father in the world. I love you. Do you have any idea how much?'

He pressed a gentle kiss to her mouth. 'I love you too, more than I can ever say, although it has to be said I'm pretty damn good at saying it now, don't you agree?'

'You are.' She kissed his mouth back. 'And I never get tired of hearing you say it.'

Vinn brushed back an imaginary hair from her face, his expression so tender and loving it made her chest expand as if her heart was searching for more room. 'I'm dying to spread the good news to Nonno and Carlotta and Rosa but there's something I have to do first.'

'What's that?'

'This,' he said, and covered her mouth with his.

* * * * *

Get 2 Free Books,
Plus 2 Free Gifts—
just for trying the Reader Service!

Get 2 Free Books,
<u>Plus</u> 2 Free Gifts -
just for trying the *Reader Service!*

Get 2 Free Books,
Plus 2 Free Gifts—

just for trying the Reader Service!